Led By Obsession

Martha Wickham

Chapter One

Deanna Jennings stood beside the sidewalk with tears on
her pink cheeks. Her short brown hair was drenched with June
sweat. Ashley Forester who lived down the end of the street
drove by in her blue station wagon and spotted Deanna. She
pulled over and stepped out. "Deanna, what's wrong?" They
had been friends for five years, ever since Deanna moved into
the block.

She acted uptight and looked tense. Her fingers shook as
she brushed her hair back. "I wanted to take a vacation. I
ordered plane tickets for myself to Hawaii from Greg, a travel
agent I met. He hasn't sent them and I was supposed to leave
tomorrow. He must have just taken my money and now I can't
get it back!"

"I'll try to get it back for you. Just give me his number and
I'll set him straight." They walked together towards Deanna's
house. Both ladies went inside.

Deanna handed Ashley her cell phone. The conversation
from what Deanna could hear didn't sound good.
Ashley looked upset. "He's denying the whole situation.
Did you keep the receipt?"

Deanna nodded in response.

"Go get it and bring it back to me. We'll have to take it to
him. I'm afraid he'll say the ticket had been nonrefundable,
but you never got a ticket. I don't know how we can prove that
yet," Ashley said.

By the time Ashley was finished talking on the phone
Deanna had the receipt in her hand. "See on the receipt it says
the ticket will be mailed out, so now we have proof. He won't
rip anyone off again! Especially not a whole five hundred
dollars like he did to me." Deanna reached in a cabinet and
pulled out a phone book. She opened it to the lawyer's section
and reached for a name that looked attractive and close to
home, the lawyer was Veronica Cane.

"Good choice," Ashley said. "We may have to threaten

this guy to get your money back."

"Ashley why don't you spend the night tonight? I'm going
to make copies of this receipt on my computer."

When all that got done the copies were put away in a folder
and the girls relaxed as the sun sunk lower in the sky releasing
colors of pink and orange against light blue. "I feel so much
better now that you're here. Thanks Ashley." Deanna lay
comfortably on the floor next to Ashley in a curled up position reading
a book.

"Let's find Greg's address in the phone book. We can go over
to his house together and maybe that would intimidate him."

"Why would you want to do that?" Ashley asked.

"To convince him to give me my money back, or a plane
ticket. I can think of all kinds of fun ways we can get revenge.
You got any?"

"Yeah, we could kidnap his dog or toilette paper his
house," Ashley suggested.

"Maybe, or we could shoot the dog or hold it for ransom."
Deanna giggled at the thought of getting revenge, which she
thought they would never do. She smiled happily and it felt
like bright sunlight bursting out from behind dark rain clouds.
Then unexpectedly there came a knock at the door. Deanna ran
back into the bedroom and shut the door.

Ashley opened the door and breathed a sigh of relief when
she saw her younger sister Sheryl. "I'm here to remind you I
want to pick up that black dress of mine you borrowed. Or you
can bring it by my house. I knew you were here because I saw
your car out front."

"Okay. Deanna and I are going camping at Pond Skinner.
Want to come?"

"Yeah, I'll meet you there."

"It's all because Deanna had been scammed by this guy
Greg and I'm trying to make it up to her."

"That rat! Tell me who he is and I'll set him straight. You know, I always wanted to be a police officer." Sheryl looked interested and aggressive.

"He's Greg Wager and he works at Travel World. We're also inviting Beth and Tara. If you see them tell them I want them to meet me at the pond." Sheryl nodded in agreement. Ashley shut the door and grabbed her cell phone to call her other two sisters to invite them. She called Tara but had to leave a message about the camping trip because no one answered.

When Ashley called Beth and told her about the trip Beth immediately became excited and accepted the invitation. While they still spoke on the phone Beth Forester took out her suitcase and opened the top. The trip would be in two days and time always seemed to go by fast for her. She packed two bags of food and got a fishing pole out of the garage.

"Don't worry about anything but driving yourself to the camp site. I'll bring all the food and after we get off the phone I'll make everyone's reservations for them." As soon as the camping reservations were made Tara called Ashley back and she also accepted the trip invitation.

Ashley spent at least an hour on the phone that evening. Deanna came back into the living room when Sheryl left and then Ashley called lawyer Veronica Cane to make an appointment. She asked for advice, "Can she sue him to get the money back?"

"If she can prove he cheated her, yes. Bring all your evidence to my office. Bring Deanna too, I want to meet her and have her fill out my questionnaire. Bring Greg's contact information. We can take him to court if we have to. Are you up to that?"

"Yes, I'll do anything to help my friend. Do you think he'll lose his job?" Ashley asked.

"Maybe if you contact his manager, which you should do," Veronica responded.

"I will, maybe he'll give her a refund. Thank you for all
your help. Can I come into your office tomorrow? Monday
we are going camping."

"Yes, so I'll see you tomorrow morning, goodbye."
Ashley tried to imagine what Veronica Cane would look
like. She might have straight shoulder length dark blond hair
and wear a dressy jacket with a skirt and act very professional
and intelligent like she knew everything about law. Ashley
giggled at the thought of guessing what Veronica would look
like and told Deanna about it.

Deanna stared and laughed. At least she felt happy.
When the evening became still Ashley decided to pack for
the camping trip. Ashley placed her cooler away in the garage,
which would be filled last. Three sleeping bags went into the
back trunk, a portable radio, matches and paper to burn, a
fishing pole with hooks, three pillows, and her cell phone. She
started to become concerned about getting Deanna to the
lawyer's office the next day. Deanna seemed willing to go so
the worry resolved.

Ashley called the travel agency to talk to the manager but
he wasn't there. The only thing left to do became waiting for
justice, but first go shopping for the camping trip, which had
been two hours away from home around a mountainside. She
imagined it being beautiful like a colorful grotto or heavenly
garden with orange monarch butterflies and the perfume of
large flowers.

The lawyers meeting took place in the morning. The
procedure had been easy and professional. The hardest part
was when they learned it would cost six hundred dollars to be
represented by Veronica. They decided it would be okay if
they both paid for half, three hundred dollars a piece. Deanna
could pay Ashley back later. After the meeting Ashley
dropped Deanna back off at home. The court case wouldn't be
for about another month with no set date yet.
Deanna had never been camping so she packed everything
she thought she would need: a cooler with food and drink,
clothes, and a book to read. She always liked nature since
childhood. Being afraid she would get bored or harassed by a
wild animal she drove over to her father's house and took his

gun. She wanted to hunt animals. Not rabbits but wolves and deer, any animal that might threaten. She also grabbed his box of bullets. They would leave in a day and she now felt ready. She grabbed her suitcase and put in her bathing suit, sun tan lotion, a jacket just in case, and blankets to sleep on. She put the gun in the suitcase also. Deanna sat on her tan couch and wished she could go to Hawaii, but decided to settle for just waiting to go to the California beach in August.

Just then the room became darker with the sunset and there came a sudden ring from the phone. Answering it quickly Deanna discovered Greg. He sounded very angry and had found out about the coming lawsuit. Deanna became nervous about the thought that he probably had her address too. Hardly listening to a word he yelled she thought about whether or not he would become dangerous and if she would soon need a restraining order. "Why are you threatening me? I didn't do anything wrong."

"Your money is nonrefundable. Now I have trouble with your lawyer and have to make time to go to court. If I don't give you the money back I could go to prison. That had better not happen to me!"

"Law is justice and it must be done. I never received my ticket and if you can't handle your business correctly there will be problems. I hope you don't do this to other customers. It will teach you to never do it again. There are more honest ways to earn a living."

"I'm warning you not to sue me. I have your address so I know where you live."

"Don't threaten me and don't come over here or I'll call the police." She finished with her phone conversation and didn't know whether to say goodbye or just hang up. She managed to mumble out a bye and hung up the phone, then unplugged it so he couldn't call back. Quickly she ran around the rooms to make sure all the doors and windows were locked.

Feeling so full of rage for his actions she plugged the phone back in and dialed the number to the travel agency. The phone rang and she hoped Greg wouldn't answer the phone. Unfortunately he did. "Travel Town this is Greg, how can I help you?"

Deanna started to hang up the phone wanting to laugh but she changed her mind asking, "Is the manager there? Can I speak to him?"

"That's Adam and he's not in."

"Will he be in soon?"

"Yes for closing tonight."

"I'll come in then."

"Is this Deanna?"

"No goodbye." She quickly hung up the phone.

When evening came Deanna went into the store asking for Adam. She looked surprised when he came to the front desk. He looked very serious and didn't smile. His had black hair and she hoped he had a heart. She explained her problem to him and he said he couldn't be sure about the refund and he would need to see her receipt. She agreed and told him about going to court with Greg. "You're going to fire him aren't you?"

"I don't think so. It may not have been his fault you didn't get the tickets. I'll investigate this problem. Maybe it got lost in the mail. I'll call you when I find anything out, I'm sure we have your number in our computer files."

Deanna became satisfied with his attempt to fix the situation. Maybe it had been an accident, either way there was a mistake and it needed to be fixed. Now her problem became keeping away from Greg because he gave her a reason to fear him. Glad he didn't show up there at that time she became tired and wanted to go home to rest. She wanted to go on the camping trip the next morning and she needed to get over to Ashley's to spend the night. At least she wouldn't be alone.

Ashley lived in Perris, California the same town as Deanna. Deanna could have walked the few blocks to her house but didn't want to. Ashley lived alone so she had an extra room for Deanna to stay in. "Did you know Greg called me and threatened me? He didn't tell me what he would do to me though. His manager isn't going to fire him either. I'll bet the lawyer will get my money back. When do you need me to pay you back?"

"When you want. We leave tomorrow morning at 10 a.m. Let's stay for five days. We are going to get dirty trust me. I'll bring soap so we can clean up in the pond. It will be fun. We need to get a small boat for the pond too. We should go out shopping again." There were a couple more things Ashley had forgotten the last time she went shopping. Not very important stuff though.

As Ashley and Deanna left that morning to go camping they anticipated the trip to be fun and peaceful. They drove for almost two hours before they came to the pond and mountain. When they arrived they looked around and studied the area. The pond looked large and grayish blue. They saw lots of grass and many tall trees that reached into the sky. Next to it sat the small mountain. Small bunches of yellow flowers grew along the side. They saw a few other tents and wanted to get as far away from them as possible. Deanna felt a little nauseated and stiff from the long drive. She breathed in the fresh country air.

They got back in the car and drove further away to the end of the pond. "The first thing we need to do is set up the tent." Ashley immediately dragged the tent out of the car and Deanna got up to help her. At that time it seemed like she thought she wouldn't enjoy this trip, but Deanna didn't say anything. The ladies set up the tent and with both their efforts it seemed easy. "Let's go for a walk and see what's around us," Ashley suggested. Deanna agreed and they walked around the pond and saw blue birds, dragonflies, ladybugs, and a little green snake.

"Look," Deanna pointed. "I'll have a hard time sleeping with him around." The snake left the area and slithered down to the other end of the pond.

The mountain was too steep to walk on being nothing but dirt and bushes. Walking back past the car the sun shone down hard and it felt hot. Both of them changed into tank tops and put on suntan lotion. Lying down on sleeping bags all they could see were peaceful, green, leafy trees. All they could hear was the whistle of the wind.

As they made lunch, peanut butter and jelly sandwiches, a fly came and landed on the cooler. Followed by another fly, then three more, and in ten minutes there were flies landing in Ashley's hair and flying and buzzing around Deanna's head. They kept trying to land on the sandwiches. Ashley even smashed one with her magazine. When the girls finished eating the flies flew away.

"Tomorrow morning we'll fish and eat them for dinner," Ashley announced.

They could see the green snake swimming in the water again, but it stayed away. They heard something bang and ran to the other side of the tent. There sat a skunk and a jug of water that had fallen off the cooler and spilled. It ran to a near by bush when it saw them and hid.

The ladies didn't want to unpack. They just arranged everything in the car where they could find it. The sleeping bags and pillows were laid out in the tent. It was quiet and all they could hear were birds and the rustling of leaves.
They both took paper cups and set them aside. They felt like picking flowers so they walked along what looked like a trail. The colors didn't match, but it looked attractive that way. The colors were yellow, orange, and purple. They were really big and twigs of leaves were added to make them look fuller.

Going back home they followed their trail and then flowers were put in water. There had been bottled juice and canned soup they cooked over a fire. The sky began to darken and both of them wondered what the night would be like. "Guess what? I brought a portable radio," Deanna pointed out.
The music played as they danced together. It played country music that sang of joy and hope. When the music stopped so did their laughter. Ashley looked and felt so full of energy she had been dying to get rid of it and she changed into her bathing suit and went swimming. Deanna joined her three minutes later and she jumped into the water.

"Don't worry, there are only harmless little fishes in here,"

Ashley claimed.

They swam close to the shore so they could stand when
they became tired. Ashley got out of the water and went to the
tent to turn on the lantern and flashlight. The sky had
darkened. The swimming went on for another ten minutes, and
then they got out and dried off. Ashley looked at her watch it
was seven in the evening. Her sisters wouldn't be there until
tomorrow afternoon at noon.

It became darker as they stared up at the sky. The moon
now looked large. It waxed into almost full. Sitting in the tent
Ashley said, "I don't want this vacation to end because on
Saturday four weeks from now we have our court case against
Greg. I'm not looking forward to that either."
It suddenly smelled like a dead animal. It was unbearable.

"Gosh Deanna what is that?"

"I don't know but I'm going outside." She grabbed a
flashlight and went out. Ashley followed her. They searched
all through the darkness and in the corner of their eyes saw a
little black animal with a white stripe run behind a bush. "Oh
it's that skunk. Does he have to ruin our air?" Deanna picked
up a pile of rocks and threw them as hard as she could at the
animal and it ran away. The horrible smell quickly dissolved.

Both of them went back into the tent. "Tomorrow we can
hunt and fish. We can pretend we're hunting Greg." Deanna
smiled before pitch dark fell. They left a tiny flashlight on for
a nightlight all night. They liked the area they were in and felt
like rulers of their own land. Ashley wanted to be a princess of
the area and meet creatures like mermaids in fresh water, or
talking cardinal birds, and fairies. She wore a crown of flowers
on her head.

Chapter Two

Beth Forester woke early to the sound of her alarm clock so she could leave for a two-hour drive to the campsite. Already packed she hurried not wanting to be late knowing her sister Ashley was waiting for her. Stiffly walking to the kitchen she realized her back and legs were sore. Then a headache came on. She shrugged her shoulders to the thought that the aches would all be gone after the vacation. She wanted one just like Deanna.

The sun came out from behind a distant horizon and when she opened the window there was nothing to be heard but the sound of birds. Excited about her second camping trip she ignored her sore muscles and practically ran to the shower.

Suddenly before getting into the shower her knees became extremely weak and she ended up taking an aromatherapy bubble bath with a lit candle trying to feel better. Day dreaming and hoping the camping area is as beautiful as it had been last time; she assumed the soreness is something a little aspirin can get rid of.

Next she tossed on something comfortable and put her suitcase and sleeping bag in her car. She didn't have her own tent but didn't mind sleeping in the bag under the trees and maybe her sister would invite her into the tent. A sharp pain pierced her back and it became more painful. So much that she didn't want to pack anything else, just a cooler for food and drink. Her head still hurt and she began to sweat. The summer heat beginning to kick in already, or was it something else?

Not having taken the aspirin yet she did so. Pond Skinner had been her camping destination and it had always been such a nice country scene she just couldn't miss it. Beth lay on her couch wishing she could sleep more and planning to do nothing but sleep and relax at the pond.

Beth pulled herself up and went to the kitchen. No reason to travel on an empty stomach. Breakfast had been light with just a plain bagel and orange juice with butter. Almost finished with her bagel she noticed her stomach's soreness. She put her plate down almost sorry she ate because the pain became worse. Walking towards her bed she bumped into the wall. Many things could have been wrong with her but she knew she was getting sick and she lay back down in her bed not wanting to get up. She knew the thermometer was only a few feet away in the bathroom so getting it would be easy.

Beth stumbled to the bathroom and placed the thermometer in her mouth for a few minutes. After taking it out of her mouth she saw her temperature read 105 degrees. Her temperature was too high she became discouraged. Not wanting to give up she still intended to leave in less than an hour though she felt awful.

As soon as that moments rest was over she stood on her feet to leave. "I'm going." Before locking the door Beth felt overwhelmingly tired again. She shook her head and walked on to her car when her eyes shut and she fainted hitting the ground hard.

When she woke again she didn't know what time it was. She then crawled back through the door and into the house lying on the living room carpet. Looking at the clock she saw she had been unconscious for an hour and a half. While staring at the ceiling it had been obvious she would be late. Her blue eyes looked faded to grey and her hair was wet with sweat and fallen out of place. All she could do was hope her problem wasn't serious Maybe she had a disease. Tears filled her eyes from disappointment. Now Beth is convinced she's sick and calls her mother to ask if she can stay with her for a while hopeful mom could cheer her up.

Immediately the phone rang and Beth just let it go. Listening to her answering machine it had been the voice of her sister Sheryl. "You must have already left. I can't wait to see you, bye."

After calling her mother Beth knew it would be best to stay with her instead of going camping. Her mother Betty lived in a large two-story house, a small farm with horses, cows and chickens. Her mother was her favorite sight when she had been sick. The support and unconditional love had been what she liked best. Leaving her car packed she waited for the strength to drive to her mother's house. Beth had been sick before and knew her body. The longer she waited to go to the doctor's office the worse her sickness could become and the harder it would be for her to drive to her mothers

Her normal routine for when she was sick had been to stay in bed, drink soda or water, and eat plenty of fruit. She started to feel very weak and wanted her mother to pick her up. Beth was hoping she really would. To be polite Beth called her sister Sheryl to let her know she wasn't going on the camping trip. "I wish you a good time," were Sheryl's last words.

With her cordless phone in hand she made three more calls. One to where she works as an assistant to a veterinarian and another to make a doctor's appointment and the last was to ask her friend Claudia for a ride to the doctor. Claudia worked with Beth at the vet's office. When that was agreed upon she pushed everything that she had in her medicine cabinet into a bag. She did it with irritation and while glancing in the mirror she saw how pale she was, but didn't bother to put makeup like she usually did.

To release some of her anger about being sick she took a tanning lamp that didn't work anymore and threw it up against the wall breaking it. Frustration swelled up in her body. The thought of seeing a counselor appealed to her then, healing her mind and her heart along with her flesh. Why had it been Beth who had to get sick and miss all the fun stuff? Her next emotion was resentment then the definite need to get a flu shot.

Looking in the mirror again all that anger had turned her face from pale to pink and she had to calm down. Standing couldn't go on and she collapsed to the floor and then crawled to the bed and fell back asleep.

An hour later she woke up to the sound of the doorbell ringing and loud knocking. Looking through the peek hole she saw Claudia waiting. "Claudia, wait just a minute!" Beth brushed her hair, rinsed her face, got her purse, and then came out the door. With little strength she made it to the car. While riding in the car Beth took four vitamins out of her purse and swallowed them without water planning to get a drink as soon as her doctor's visit ended.

"Thanks for coming and getting me. I appreciate it."

"I'll drop you off then come pick you up after an hour."
Claudia looked serious. She always seemed to be thinking and
worrying about something, but her brown eyes constantly
seemed extra friendly.

Beth didn't talk because she was too sick. All she could
say was, "Thanks, bye," and Claudia drove away. After
checking in at the nurses' desk she sat down. She had not been
very patient in waiting rooms and luckily the nurse called her
name to go back to the doctor's office quickly. Her doctor's
name was Joe Daniels and she always went to him when she
got sick. "I want a flu shot as soon as I can get one."
The nurse nodded then took Beth to the doctor's and left
the room.

Beth watched the doctor as he closely looked her over. "It
could be the, flu, or food poisoning."

"I want you to go to the hospital. They can tell you what
type of food poisoning you have. As Long as it's not botulism
you'll be okay. We don't give flu shots until the winter so
come back in November. This probably isn't the flu. Try to
remember what you ate in the last week and I'll give you this
prescription and note to take to the hospital. They'll know
what to do with you." The visit was over quickly. Beth called
Claudia to come get her sooner and her mother to inform her to
pick her up that night.

"I'm convinced it's food poisoning." Beth was still sick
riding back home in the car with Claudia. "Thanks for the ride.
I would have walked but I don't have the strength." When she
arrived home she went right to bed where she would stay until
her mother picked her up the next morning.

Sheryl Forester sat next to her packed suitcase ready to
leave for the camping trip. Feeling aggravated she couldn't
quit thinking about Deanna's problem. Sheryl loved her sisters
and couldn't let Ashley deal with the problem herself. She
always agreed with Ashley. Quickly she grabbed her keys off
the counter and got into her car to drive to Greg's. She had
gotten his address from the phonebook. He lived in the town
of Victorville, California.

Two hours and thirty minutes later Sheryl pulled up to a

desolate, dirty, old looking large grey house. Even the trees looked worn. When she knocked on the door Greg answered it immediately.

He looked like he didn't want to talk to her and shut the door almost completely.

"Are you Greg Wager?"

He nodded. There were voices of people talking behind him.

"I didn't mean to bother you if you have company. I just want to talk to you for a minute."

"It's okay it's just me. The voices are only my TV."

"Anyway, did you already know Deanna didn't get her tickets before she told you she didn't? And why can't you refund the money if she never received them? Once you lose in court you will have to pay her. I want you to be ready. We should have your manager in court too since we're suing the business not you personally. Do you want to give me the money now and save trouble?"

Greg stepped out of the door and nodded. "I'm sorry for all of the inconvenience. Deanna does look tense and really needed a vacation. I'm so embarrassed for my mistake. Why don't you come in while I get my checkbook?"

Sheryl smiled and bounced up and down acting victorious and went into his house. She sat down on his brown leather couch in what appeared to her to be his living room. The summer air was thick and dusty. His ceiling fan blew warm air and a faucet started to drip. Her face began to drip with sweat and she stood up. "What's taking so long?" She sat back down.

"You think I'm slow? I mean, I thought I sent the stupid tickets out! For all we know this is the post office's fault! You should contact them. I'm not giving you money until this is investigated."

"But I can't. You need to."

"No I don't and I won't. So what will you try next to get
that money? I hope you don't have to get really bad. My
cousin told me your family acted like that. You do seem to
appear that way also."

Sheryl's face turned pink with heat and anger. Pushed to
the limit she refused to be insulted and quickly punched him in
the mouth.

Greg ran to stand in the way of the front door. Getting
around him seemed impossible. There is a sudden sense in the
air that she has felt her eternity in that spot. Would he ever let
her leave? If he did when would that be? Would it be soon
enough? A wave of fear and regret shot through her body from
head to toe. Her head glanced around the room looking at the
small windows that appeared to be her only way out.
He did not look angry and smiled. As if all the tension had
been appealing to him. He stepped toward her and grabbed her
by her hair.

"You're wrong to do this. You have to show up in court.
If you don't the police will arrest you! If they don't Deanna
and Ashley would make sure they do. I know my sister and
you'll be sorry." At that time she noticed he also held on to her
arm. "Are you going to let go of me? If you're not giving me
the money I have to go."

"Why? Tell me." He squeezed tighter.

"Ashley and Deanna are camping at Pond Skinner. I am
meeting them there today."

"Oh yeah? Need me to give you a ride?"

"No, I have my own car." Sheryl looked frightened.
Worked out to her last drop of energy she stopped trying to
struggle out of his grasp. He watched Sheryl quickly reach into
her purse and yank out a gun. She used this chance to back up
away from him and he didn't come towards her. She stood
there still not firing her gun. Sheryl usually didn't carry a gun.
She had taken the gun out of a fear of camping with wild
animals. It had wasn't even purchased but borrowed without
permission from her father's cabinet.

Greg's Cousin Caleb was hiding in another room and came up behind her and hit her on the head with a wrench. Sheryl fell to the ground unconscious. Her mind relaxed in a state that had been much like sleep to her, but she had completely fainted.

Immediately Greg took her arms and his cousin took her ankles and they carried her up to the attic. They laid her on a dusty blue couch, took her gun, and shut the door. It did not lock from the outside. "I'm almost glad she fainted. I was afraid she was going to shoot me for a minute." Greg stated. His cousin took and held the small black gun. "I want to shoot her. What right does she have pointing this at you?"

"No you can't, and you've just made a point but then what right do you have pointing it at her?" Greg argued. "Besides, she's already unconscious and you don't want to be a murderer. I see those kinds of people on TV and they all live in regret, guilt, and fear of prosecution. When they are caught they must be locked away which doesn't look like much fun."

"She is kind of pretty. With a makeover she'd be even better. Do you think she would go out with me?" asked Caleb.

"No, you're joking right?" Greg asked.

"I guess so. Should we call an ambulance? What do we do now?"

"We'll take her out to Pond Skinner or the mountain and leave her there. We'll hide her car in the backyard right now." They walked down the stairs. "I still want to shoot her though," I've never killed anyone before added Caleb. Greg didn't know if Caleb was serious or not. "Her car is right out front so we need to move it now." Greg watched Caleb sit down.

Caleb reached over a small table and opened a beer. He took a drink.

"You can't sit down. You need to help me."

"You need me to help you move it. Go ahead, here are the keys." He tossed them to Greg. "Why don't you want anyone to know she's here?"

"Why do you think? Look at what we just did. She'll be missing and I'm assuming if someone finds the car they'll accuse us. Her family will get angry and we'll be in trouble."

"We'll be in trouble if she goes home. What now?" Caleb asked.

"She can't do anything. She won't be able to prove we did this." Greg walked outside by himself to move the car. After starting it he drove it to the backyard. Now he needed to hide its appearance. There were grey clouds in the sky and a hard wind starts to blow his long black hair in his face. The only place to hide it was behind his large shed and he covered it with blankets. The garage was out of the idea because there already were two cars in it and boxes of old stuff. Greg thought it would also be one of the first places an officer would look.

When the car is covered the wind begins to blow again and the blanket starts to come off. Greg gathered up ten large rocks to hold the blanket down in place. "It would have been easier if Caleb had been here to help me." Greg couldn't wait to get in out of the wind and he walked up to Sheryl in the attic.

Caleb came up behind him.
Going in they saw that she was not awake but breathing.
Caleb took a small rope and tied her hands behind her back.
"How are we going to lock her in here?"

"I don't know. I don't think we can. Maybe we should call the police."

"On ourselves?"

"No."

"But what if we went to jail? We can't can we?" asked Caleb. This all had been a mistake. We are not really bad people."

"We don't want to hurt her. Let's take her back home."
Though most people had treated Greg like a mean person he

did have a small soft spot in his heart. It was his family that gave him a bad reputation. His father and Caleb were both into crime. Many times Greg wanted to steal because he could have gotten away with it. But seeing Deanna's sad disappointed face had been too much for him and he really wanted to help get her money. He wanted to make sure this mistake would never happen again.

"No, we should keep her for ransom. It'll be fun keeping her."

"Caleb, how can we? She'll run. We can't keep her in the attic for the rest of her life."

"I'll give us 24 hours to come up with an idea."

"I'm going to call the police and tell them what happened." Greg ran to the phone in his room and locked the door behind him and dialed the number to the local police. Greg said nothing.

"What now?" Caleb asked as Greg came out.

"They told me to drive her home. I don't even know where the wench lives. Maybe we'll find her driver's license. Where the heck is her purse? They said they will stop by tonight to see if everything's okay. What if Sheryl needs to go to the hospital?" Greg could tell by the way the officer rushed the call that the office had been busy that day. Maybe it was too hectic for them.

They drove out on the highway for thirty minutes then stopped at an area where there was nothing around but longs, yellow grass, and a body of water that had been nameless. Sheryl lay in the back of the car still out. Her face was pale. The area was quiet enough for them to lay her down in some tall grass. They hoped someone would find her there and she would become someone else's problem.

"I want her gun," said Caleb.

"It's not yours you shouldn't," Greg replied.

"She attacked you so it's mine now."

"Just drive the car okay Greg.

"What are you going to do with that thing?" Greg asked.

"Uh," Caleb looked as though he had been thinking of an answer. "Hunt animals."

"What for?"

"For sport or to sell their fur."

"Don't let the humane society hear you say that." Evening began to fall and as they drove down the highway Greg turned on his car lights.

Sheryl did nothing but lay in the dirt unconscious. The men didn't even have the decency to lay her on a blanket. The sky still seemed to be cloudy not clearing up and tiny sprinkles began to cover her body. It picked up faster and faster until it became heavy rain.

"It rained last night," Greg pointed out in the morning.

"Feeling remorseful he wanted to go back and see what happened to Sheryl.

When they both approached the scene Sheryl had been lifeless for some time laying face down in a puddle. There was mud everywhere and the area seemed to have become a graveyard. It looked desolate like a brown swamp and black birds flew around it landing to perch on branches. It seemed completely different and transformed since they had seen the area the day before. It went from a golden valley to a gray swamp. Both men had the look of oops we made a mistake on their faces. Caleb turned her over. She was dead and both of them wanted to believe she died by her own sword, from her own aggression.

Sheryl did not look scary and ugly but peaceful and pretty like Snow White in a glass case. The wind begins to blow hard again and dirt swirled around like mini tornados. This began to dry her clothing, but dirt and dead fallen leaves were blown everywhere covering her. It became afternoon and the small storm passed them by.

The men did not want to take her or leave her there. "Let's leave her here. She's already dead," Caleb suggested. As they started to leave rain drops began to fall again as they drove away. "We're not going back now. Maybe we'll make an anonymous call to the cops."

Chapter Three

Ashley and Deanna sat innocently in the shade of the trees.
"I see everyone's decided to ditch our camp." Ashley noticed
nobody had showed up. It was thirty minutes past the time the
sisters were supposed to show up. "I wish I had my cell phone,
and then I would call and see where they are. It would be more
fun if they were here." Her skin had become a light
brownish pink that she had just soaked up from the sun earlier.

Now the sun was gone and a rainy mist began to fall.
Both ladies ran to the car and sat down inside. Just then the
mist turned to rain again. Not wanting to stand in the rain they
watched it pour over their tent.

When an hour went by time really dragged slowly in the
car. "I wish I would have known it would rain," Ashley
whispered. Looking angry she pulled the car out of the mud
and drove to the road. "What motel do you want to stay at?"
"How about the Pond Inn?" Deanna asked.

In agreement Ashley said, "That motel might be cool. It's
so cute like a cabin."

Only after spending one night at the motel the rain had
stopped and they went back to their tent. "I'm surprised it's
still here." The sun started to shine on them as Deanna opened
the tent zipper and water came pouring out. Everything on the
campsite was grimy with mud.

Quickly they tossed everything into the trunk of the car and
then drove around looking for dry areas. They didn't find any
until they actually came to another town. There weren't any
road signs so they didn't know what town they were in. There
were abandoned wooden houses and buildings they wanted to
stay in.

Everything got taken out of the car and laid in the sun to
dry. They spread their tent out over a wooden banister also.
Noticing a large, old empty Inn Deanna fell in love with it and
wanted to stay there. She took her suitcase out and ran upstairs
to an empty room leaving it there.

Ashley stepped into the house to join her. "It's like you really love this place. Too bad you can't buy it. I'm running back to the motel to make phone calls to let my sisters know where we are. Do you want to come?"
Deanna shook her head no.

"I'll be back soon, bye."

Deanna searched around the room looking for something to engage in while Ashley was gone. There was only one thing left to do and that was to explore.

Deanna stepped outside and saw mud turning to dirt. Dirt blew past her face in the wind. Looking up to the sky she could see the clouds were visibly moving to the east leaving the area. The sun felt warm. She had been enchanted by the whole area and noticed what looked like an old wooden store.

After walking over she tried the door and it opened. There wasn't much left there but the counter and an old fashioned register. She could hear the wind whistling through the cracks in the wood.

Walking through the store she found, in the back, what looked like an old dusty bedroom. As if someone had once lived there. A loud noise that sounded like a shot gun blast came from the nearby trees making her very curious to see what did it and she ran outside away from the deserted town.

Ashley pulled up in her car and went inside the abandoned Inn. "Deanna, I got a hold of Beth but no one else. I left a message with my mother though." She gasped. It frightened her to realize Deanna wasn't there. "Deanna!" She called over and again but no one answered. Frustrated Ashley threw herself on an old mattress.

The whole trip had been her idea so she wanted to pretend to be having a great time. Why not? It couldn't have been that bad. Ashley looked forward to building a fire and roasting hot dogs and marshmallows, which had been what she intended on doing that night. She crossed her fingers that Deanna would come home before dark and left them there for an hour. To help time pass she began to clean up the Inn. Still there was no sign of Deanna.

Tara Forester drove along a solitary mountain to get to Pond Skinner late. She planned to go a day later but never went before because she couldn't take time off work. After receiving a call from Ashley she headed towards the ghost town. She had been given directions but not the name of the town. Still driving 20 minutes away from her destination she saw the road was covered with rocks, thorns, and fallen branches from the rain. Noticing this she drove over it slowly.

After an ear piercing pop sound she felt her car sink lower. Her tires were dragging. The car slowed down and became difficult to control and turning a corner she slid off the road and stopped at a tree stump hitting it. She opened the car door spending the first amount of her time relaxing. Not a single car was seen driving by. It soon became hotter in the car so she stepped out and to check the front of her car. There was only a small dent.

Inspecting the tires she saw they were covered with road trash, mud, and two of them were flat. Looking closer she also noticed thorns, many of them. Tara assumed they were blown in the road by the earlier storm. As time slowly went by she sat on the ground and waited for a car to drive by. She hoped maybe by a miracle it would be her sister, Ashley, or her mother. Aggravation led her to hand pick the thorn bunches out. Still no one drove by. She began to pull them out faster until one pinched her finger and it lightly bled. Reaching into her trunk she took a brick of ice out of her cooler and placed her finger on it.

Taking her purse out of her car she searched for her cell phone. It was not there. It was not where she had left it. Feeling desperate because no cars passed by she began to walk back towards home. Though she had been 30 minutes from her residence it had been worth the effort and with her purse around her shoulder and her suitcase pulled by its wheels Tara hoped maybe she would lose a few pounds.

After walking up along the mountainside Tara became tired and sat down on her suitcase. Quickly sitting up she spotted a man riding up the road on a bike. She began waving her arms wildly yelling "Hey!"

He rode over to her. "Do you need help? I'm riding to the mini mart and I want a drink."

"There's a mini mart down this lonely road?"

"The mart is 20 minutes down this road on a bike. Are you lost?"

"No, I have two flat tires on my car and no phone to use."

"Is this is an emergency? My house is back down off this road. You want to use my phone?"

Feeling beat and desperate she agreed.

"Let's go then. The address is 301 Pine drive. It's the only house on the side of the mountain," he explained. He began walking with his bike and she followed.

"I'm supposed to be camping with my sister but I've missed it." She approached the road sign Pine drive. The grey house was so large it had been visible from the start of the road. It was two levels and as wide as a small shopping mall.

The many trees created shadows all around them and Tara became nervous about her new surroundings. The trouble of the day was starting to get to her. She offered conversation.

"What's your name? I'm Tara Forester. My sisters call me Tiara."

"Nice to meet you, I'm Kenny Walker." They continued to walk and he opened the front door. It was unlocked.

"You leave your front door unlocked?" She asked.

"Usually because I'm used to nobody being out here."
Tara looked at him like okay and he signaled with his hand for her to go inside.

"You can sit down here," he said as he handed her a phone.

They were in his study room. The carpet was red and the couch was velvet blue but the walls were only brown.

Tara sat down on the couch. "You live alone?"

"Yes."

"Why live in such a large house?"

"Well, it belonged to my family. When my grandparents died they left it to me."

"It's gorgeous."

"Thank you."

"May I admire it?" She asked meaning can she look around.

He agreed to let her.

Looking out the kitchen window she saw it was still damp out. The ground was dark brown and the black metal fence was all wet.

"Are you from Victorville originally?" he asked.

She turned around and saw him standing in the doorway. "No I was born in San Diego. I grew up there. I've called and they said they'd come get my car and then I'll go. Sorry I interrupted your bike ride."

His young face looked optimistic. "That's okay there's always tomorrow and every day after that to go riding."

"The company said they'd be here as soon as possible."

"While we're waiting, would you like a drink with crackers and cheese?"

Tara wondered if he had been trying to flirt with her. "Yes, thank you." *Fine as long as he didn't put cyanide in it,* she thought. "Where are your parents?"

"They're spending the summer in Seattle." He left the room and Tara assumed it was to get the snacks as he promised.

In an hour it became darker outside and Tara's tow truck still hadn't come. She finished up her crackers with Swiss cheese and wine.

"You can spend the night to wait for the tow truck. There are plenty of rooms here. Besides the damn rain storm might come back." Kenny had a look of concern.

"Okay great." She was glad to get to stay in the mansion. She always wanted her own palace.

"I'll let you choose which room you want to stay in. Go ahead," he said trying to be nice.

"Thank you."

"It's always a pleasure to meet new young ladies." He kissed her hand.

She picked up her suitcase and rolled it around the house looking for a room. This house was unique because many of the rooms had different colored carpet. She chose the room with dark green painted walls. The room had been decorated in green and it made it seem like a tropical paradise or a year round Christmas room. There were two houseplants, and a fireplace. It was perfect. She took a lighter out of her purse and placed it by the fireplace so she could light a fire if rain started, though the room was not cold.

That night the house was very dark and she did not know where Kenny had gone. There was no light and Tara was feeling out in front of her to help her find her way. When she found the kitchen she opened the door and saw a mouse run by.

Feeling so tired it fascinated her, the animal was found in a corner. She tried to pet its soft fur but in a second it rolled over and bit her. Blood ran from her finger and it dripped. She ran to the sink and washed it off. While bending over the sink Tara realized her legs were sore and walking out to her car was not a possibility. Out of frustration Tara hurried back to her room and sat down.

Kenny appeared in her doorway. He studied her because

she had changed into a brown silky nightgown. "Don't go to sleep. We don't want you to miss the tow truck."
When he left Tara collapsed on her bed at the thought of staying up all night waiting for a tow truck. After staring at the ceiling for ten minutes she fell asleep.

Sunlight lit up Tara's room. Jumping up she ran out into the house looking for Kenny. When she didn't find him she knew the last place she didn't look would be the area where he was. He was in the kitchen eating. Tara wondered why she didn't look there first. "Can I have more crackers and cheese?" she asked smiling.

"This morning you can have anything you want. Help yourself to the kitchen. I wouldn't want to starve you with just crackers."

Tara began looking in all the cabinets. "Why isn't the tow truck here?"

"Didn't you tell them to meet you here? They won't. You should have been waiting by your car. You should call them again and wait by your car. We'll do this. We'll drive over and put your car in neutral and push it into this driveway. It shouldn't be too hard and it will save you some money. It's really not that far. What else can we do? Or I'll help you back it out and you can slowly drive it up here."

"Okay, can I use your phone? I want to call my mother."
He agreed and asked, "Where do you live again? I forgot."

"In Victorville, in a rented one bedroom home is all. It's all I have for now."

"If you really like it here I can rent you a room for only one hundred dollars a month."

"Thanks, I'll consider it. I can't believe I drove over thorns from the storm. My sister Ashley wanted to take her friend Deanna on a camping trip because of this big stress and fraud problem she has. My sister has to go to court with her in a week. I don't think she wants to go."

"You want to drive by Pond Skinner and see if we can find

her?" he asked.

"No, I feel sorry for her though because it rained. It's like
she has this string of bad luck. My sister's a workaholic like a
manager, always into her store. Ashley must want to work her
way up to the top."

"What is that blood on the floor?"

"I found a mouse last night and it bit me." Tara showed
him the bruised finger. "I couldn't find any band-aids."

"They're in one of the bathroom cabinets. I'll get you
one." Kenny left the room but didn't come back. Tara had
been starting to feel at home there and wanted to take
advantage of his rental deal. Her impression of him was that
he was a younger, attractive, friendly man who made her feel
safe. His slim muscular build looked extremely confident.

Going back into the bedroom she found him sitting on the
bed with a band-aid and peroxide. "Hi, what is it you do for a
living? I'm a florist; I make all kinds of flower arraignments
for special occasions. I love working with flowers because
they're so pretty. It makes me feel good to put something
together that will become a gift or brighten up a sick persons
day."

"That's nice," Kenny said. "I am a real estate agent and
when I graduate from college I hope to be a lawyer."

"You seem smart enough. I'd like to take you up on your
rental deal. Nothing's better than getting a roommate. After
we get my car can I pay you then move in as soon as I want?"

"Of course you can." He held out his hand and she shook
it. It was considered a friendship gesture.

"First I'm going to clean up that blood then I'll get ready to
go get the car." Tara ran off in a surge of excitement.

Deanna stood in the middle of the forest clearing. She saw
the sun looked lower in the sky and she knew it was later in the
afternoon. A light fog blew across the pine trees and she heard
a strange noise. She walked around looking for what it could

have been. At that moment Deanna felt silly that she had chased after that loud sound. Figuring she would never find it she started walking back to the town. The sound made her feel frightened. It seemed mysterious and she wanted to walk back faster.

As the sun became lower in the sky the area didn't seem so cute any more but now it scared her. "I'm glad it's not midnight." All the standing and walking made her tired and she sat down to rest. Cushioned by soft green leaves she lay down and closed her eyes.

"Deanna," Ashley called. Deanna had been too far away to hear the call. Ashley stomped back into the home and tried to lock the door. The lock did not work. She wanted to stay and wait a day and if Deanna didn't come back she would call the police. "Come on Dee, there's wild animals out there," Ashley said as she sat down on the wood floor.

The old house had no electricity and no water. Ashley felt glad she brought jugs of water. Ashley began looking through Deanna's suitcase and found her gun. She checked to make sure it was loaded and then put it in the desk drawer. They weren't planning on telling scary stories that night. Her heart throbbed and her face flushed pink. Her eyes filled up with tears. "Deanna, please tell me you're still out picking flowers."

By nighttime Ashley had their flashlight on. An eerie hard wind blew. This wind strangely seemed to have its own intelligence to Ashley like it knew where it wanted to go.

"Deanna!"

Deanna walked through the door not holding flowers. Ashley ran to hug her and immediately it was obvious she had been worried about Deanna. They both were somewhat afraid and uncomfortable so they both tried to sleep in the same room. A scratching sound started on the walls and by midnight it was still there but louder. The wind was blowing and a metal can rolled past them. Ashley called her mother on her cell phone.

"Where are you?" Darlene asked.

"We are fifteen miles north of pond Skinner in an abandoned town. We're trying to sleep in an Inn."

"I know where you are. That's Bodie. A ghost town." Neither of them could fall asleep and they got their bags together to leave. After running to the car they drove back to the same old campsite they were at by Pond Skinner. They arrived in the same spot and they slept all night in their sleeping bags and didn't wake up until the next afternoon.

"Only one more night here and you won't look as tense as you did when we first started." Ashley knew Deanna's tense look when she saw it.

"Sorry I scared you back at that deserted town."

"That's okay, at least I didn't have to use your gun."

"What will we do today?"

"Everything a couple camping girls would do."

"We've been camping so long."

"Let's celebrate our last night out here." Ashley knew exactly what she would do.

After snacking on cinnamon rolls that were heated over a low fire they covered themselves in sun tan lotion, changed into their bathing suites, and jumped into the pond. They swam for exercise and to cool themselves off. Minutes later they were out and lying on towels to dry. Both ladies were pleased about the amount of sun they absorbed.

"Time for us to catch dinner." Ashley announced and both of them laughed. While walking to the other end of the pond they took fishing poles, and a can filled with muddy worms. They found these worms themselves by digging under muddy rocks. They sat on rocks sipping juice, put the worms on a hook with gloves on, and tossed their fishing lines as far out into the water as they could.

Ashley had the first bite but when she reeled it in it was only a small fish they did not want to eat so she threw it back.

In an hour they had both caught their own rainbow trout. Quickly they were cleaned with hunting knives and washed with a jug of water. When they got back to camp Ashley started the fire they would cook the fish over. They planned to eat them with tartar sauce and ranch dressing.

By the time they were finished cooking the fish it was dinnertime and their meals turned out well. They even added fruits and vegetables to their plates and carrots had been tossed in while they cooked with the fish in foil.

"I brought cupcakes," Ashley said as she showed them covered in plastic cups. She took them out, put candles on them, and lit them. "You get to make yourself a wish then blow it out."

After they both blew out their candles Deanna said, "My wish was I hope Greg loses the court case and he never takes anyone's money again."

"I hope the rest of this vacation is a smooth paradise. I know there's only one night left but that could mean a lot." Ashley looked relaxed but worried. "Let's roast hot dogs tonight. I love fire burn on my hot dog."

As Ashley began to light the fire again she said, "Dean, your tickets were legally non-refundable. That's a rule by travel agents because it's that airlines rule." The fire made popping sounds. "I saved this information Veronica Cane told me because I wanted you to enjoy this vacation. You'll have to get your tickets from them by using what you bought as credit towards future travels, but not the whole price. I know Greg unfairly did this to you and maybe we can get $100.00 from him in court but that will only reimburse us a little for the price we'll pay for the lawyer. I know it seems like Greg is getting away with this. Maybe it could be considered stealing. Do you think he did this on purpose? Have you ever taken a vacation on a plane before?"

"I've never taken a plane to go on vacation before. I'm not sure if he had been trying to take advantage of me. He's definitely displaying negligence."

"The manager found your ordering info on their computer

though. I asked why they didn't find it before your trip date passed. They said it had been your fault for not showing up at the airport. I knew they should have better informed someone like you what was going on. I have a bad feeling about this Greg Wager guy and I wish you had picked a different travel agency. Next time just buy your damn ticket from the airline online. It's so easy. Greg is just a bad travel agent. With the way he's acting I'm sure he won't finish out the year working for them. I don't think you'll need a lawyer. We can cancel this if you would like, unless you want to try press charges."

Deanna sat silently. "Thanks for your help." She lay down to rest as she watched Ashley put two hot dogs on steal pokers. When evening came sounds were heard from the forest. Wanting to go home Deanna sat resting staring at the sky watching the first faded star that began to shine. "What are those noises?" A dinging sound repeated itself and there was a scuffling sound. "I hope that isn't a bear."

The sky grew darker and Deanna brightened her lantern. The dinging sound started again. Deanna picked up her gun and Ashley followed her toward the sound. It led them to a bush. Deanna pointed her gun at it. She pulled the trigger twice shooting the bush. The sound had stopped. They stepped closer to the bush to see what it had been. Not once did they think it was a person and it wasn't. A skunk lay there dead and it was covered in blood. An open can of soup laid next to it, which explained the dinging sound. Neither of them expected what happened next.

A horrible smell pierced the night air. It drowned out the smell of pine, fish, and wild daisies. They tried to get away from it by moving to the tent but there had been no escape.

"Now what do we do?" Deanna asked.

"We should burn it, bury it, and then move south." Ashley pointed to 30 feet away down a trail.

They scooped up the skunk with a garbage bag and took it down to the other side of the pond. They tossed it on a burning fire and while it burned they dug a hole with their hands and spoons. During that time the air began to clear. The ashes and wood were scooped up by Ashley and tossed into the hole.

When they were finished the sky was dark and their
lanterns glowed brightly. There was a pack of animals howling
in the distance that they assumed were wolves. After washing
their hands in the pond they gave up on the idea of moving the
tent and they both sat down.

The moon became almost full and it lit up the area. They
heard only silence until a breeze blew the leaves and it made
rustling sounds. "I almost don't want to go back home,"
Ashley said. "Let's move away. The sight of Greg's face will
probably make me sick. We can go to New Mexico. There's a
vet's office there that would possibly hire me."

"Are you serious?"

"Yes, we could be roommates and that would split our
living costs in half."

"Good idea. I'll see what I can do."
"Let me know in the morning because I want to go now.
You should get all your stuff and move in with me first before
we leave."

The day was over and they both were trying to sleep. The
area was beautiful with green. The grass was tall and trees that
seemed to protect them from intruders surrounded them. On
the right side of the blue tent were daisy flowers separated in
rows of color by nature. The first row was yellow, the second
orange, and the third purple. They felt welcome by the wild
forest.

Ashley knew Deanna had been sleeping with a gun but
didn't understand it. Why was she so afraid? Was it Greg or
the skunk? Deanna had earlier expressed that she couldn't wait
to leave but Ashley did not want to go, she wanted to build a
log cabin out there and retreat like in a far off convent. The
sounds and scent of nature could have been bought in a candle
or audiotape but she had all the relaxation right there. Even the
fresh air felt good in her lungs. Ashley closed her eyes and
drifted off.

Deanna opened her eyes and stared at her gun. In a second
the roof of the tent had caved in and was covering the both of
them. She could tell something obviously laid on it and it

frightened her so she grabbed her gun and shot it. Ashley woke and jumped up. Quickly they both crawled out the front and ran away. Looking from a short distance they saw it had been only a thick heavy branch that fell off a tree when the breeze blew. There was a hole in the roof of the tent now but lucky for them it would not rain again. "I think we should go back to the hotel now," Deanna added sarcastically.

Deanna watched Ashley as she quickly pushed the branch off and popped the tent back up to go back to sleep. They were able to rest peacefully the remainder of the night though they both heard sounds like leaves and insects. A soft wind started blowing again and kept blowing. To Deanna she agreed it had been beautiful but was annoying.

Deanna did not want to get up and by the time she woke it was almost time to leave. Trying to find the motivation to move she laid a towel down and bathed in the sun. Before packing and loading her belongings in the car she took a sharp knife out of her purse and she went to pick a bouquet of wild flowers.

Soon Ashley saw her walking back with a bunch of flowers.

"I don't want to see Greg ever again," Deanna pointed out.

"Don't worry; we'll be safe in the court room if we decide to go on with that." Ashley was trying to look comforting by acting relaxed.

"Are you sure I could win?"

"Yes because you're right, you should win. If you don't the judge is wrong."

Acting assured Deanna went in the tent and took her camera to take last minute pictures of the area. She thought it was beautiful because there were so many trees and flowers. Ashley started loading up the car. Deanna came to help her take down the tent. "Say your final goodbye to this area. Bye."

Deanna said her goodbyes also.

"Let all your stress go now, melting off your body. Leave it here."

Deanna nodded and they put the tent in the back of the car. It was the last of their things to be loaded and they both got in the car and drove away.

Chapter Four

"I want to know what happened to my sisters. I'm calling
them right now." Ashley said as she sat down next to Deanna.

"Forget calling them, they're never home."
Deanna moved over to a brown couch across the room and
laid down to close her eyes. The house was quiet.
The sound of a knock pounded on the door and Ashley
glanced out the window. The knock came from her mother.

When she opened the door her mother walked in.
"Hi Ashley, did you enjoy your camping trip?" Her mother
lowered her voice into a whisper when she saw Deanna
sleeping on the couch. "All of you sisters wanted to go
camping but Beth is at my house getting over food poisoning
and Tiara got a flat tire and had to stay with some strange boy
and Sheryl, I don't know. We can't find her anywhere."

"I should go see them."

"Sheryl hasn't been seen in so long. She's missing and the
police are almost ready to start an official search. She's only
seventeen and never just disappeared before. But I'm most
angry about the fact that she's missing school. I want you to
come over to my house. There is so much room. I'd like a
reunion while Sheryl's missing so we can all look and pray for
her together. Will you come stay with me? Your friend can
stay here and she can watch your house for you. It won't be
for too long." I'm sure she'll just come home soon.

"Okay, I just want to go over to Tara's house now to check
on her. Do you want to ride there with me?"

"No that's okay. I want to get home in case Sheryl calls."
Tara came outside to greet her sister. "Sorry I missed
camping. My car is in the shop and I'm getting new tires. My
new roommate is coming to pick me up and I have plans with a
real estate agent to sell this house. I'll be better off staying
with him. He has a beautiful house. I'll invite you over and
you can see it. It's just like moms except without all the
candles. Want to know more about him? He is so nice. His
name is Kenny Walker. I think he's rich and he won't admit it.

I met him when I had a flat tire. Do you think that's bad?"

"No, I don't."

"At least you'll be safe from Greg."

"There's a Greg out there? My car will be ready in a few days. Will you take me to pick it up?"

"Yes, I promise."

"Good, thanks."

"I'm glad you're okay. I have to go because Sheryl's disappeared and I am going to stay with mom to help her take care of Beth and look for Sher. I'll see you later. Call me if you need me, bye."

Tara watched Ashley drive away. She felt unfortunate bad things were happening but then she had been grateful that in the middle of it all she realized how much she loved her sisters and that she had made a new great friend in Kenny.

Ashley passed by Sheryl's house only to find that she still didn't come home. A police officer's car passed by her watching the area. He had been watching for Sheryl's return. To Ashley it seemed everyone knew in the towns of Victorville and Perris that Sheryl Forester had disappeared. Veronica Cane, Deanna's lawyer, also knew because that had been the reason her appearance in court along with Greg had been canceled. The police had it in their records that the last time Sheryl had been seen was the day Ashley left to go camping. With hopeful hearts they all assumed and told each other Sheryl had taken off somewhere with someone she knew well and had been having too much of a good time to call.

When arriving at her mother's home Ashley saw that her mother's answering machine was always on in case Sheryl called. Why hadn't she called? Ashley's mother glided around the house like nothing was wrong and performed an, I don't care worry act. Ashley also worried, and she wondered where Greg Wager was. Her intuition told her something was wrong.

"Why do things seem so weird all the sudden? It's Greg, he must be bad luck," Ashley told her mother feeling melancholy. She went up the stairs to Beth's room to check on her.

Beth looked better. She was resting and she sat up in bed when Ashley came in her room. Beth was weak and pale, however she was feeling better.

"The medication is working I see," Ashley said as she picked the dirty clothes up off of the floor. After Beth's look of agreement Ashley asked, "Are you sure you're not pregnant?" Ashley looked at the floor as if a good joke had just gone bad.

"Is there anything you need?" Ashley asked.

"No, when is mom leaving? I need her."

"Don't worry, not until tomorrow. I'll be bringing your meals to you and I think you need another doctor's appointment. I'll schedule one for you. As your big sister who loves you I want to make sure you know what's going on with Sheryl. She's missing and I have a seriously bad sense here, just promise me that when you get better you won't go and talk to or argue with Greg."

"I promise you." Beth had been honest. The temptation to disobey her sister was there and Greg suddenly seemed like a very creepy person.

"When would you like your doctor's appointment?"

"Tomorrow would be good because I feel myself getting better quickly but I don't want to relapse and I'm almost finished with my medication. Maybe I'll need a refill."

"That's fine; if that's what you want then that's what you'll have. Does mom know what you want for dinner? I'll bring you desert too since you're sick. Do you think you can eat now?"

"I want soup and no desert for a while though, thanks."
Beth's eyes became weak and started to shut.

Ashley closed the curtains to create darkness for Beth to sleep in and she left the room quietly. The upstairs had become Beth's own home so Ashley stayed in a room near her mother's downstairs in the right corner of the house. Picking up a brown old-fashioned telephone she called Deanna. "I forgot to give you the phone number here."

"That's alright. I'm canceling the court case for good."

"Why?"

"So you can stay with your mother as Long as you need to do so."

"Can't you do it without me? You should. I want you to take him to court and beat his ass. Sheryl is missing and I have a sick feeling about Greg. I'm afraid of him. This could be our only chance for community safety and justice. I'm sure you'll regret it if you don't. You can't let him get away. Come on Deanna you can do it, just call me if you need me."

"Okay for you I will. I'll reschedule the court date as soon as I can."

"Yes and do it for yourself also. Veronica is a great lawyer. Goodnight Deanna and good luck." Ashley hung up. The whole house had been so quiet she didn't think her mother was home. She lay down on her bed to think and relax but she was still upset. Any strange sound in that house would have frightened her. "No," Ashley said to herself. "The strange sounds will wait to come out at midnight tonight." She hoped the only sounds she would hear would be of Beth getting better.

"I can't believe Sheryl would just run off like this!" Ashley swung her arms in the air with frustration. She had rejected the thought of life becoming a nightmare. She flung her arms around as if she was smacking the problem out of sight. "Tara's car breaks down, Beth got food poisoning, Sheryl's is gone now, and it rained on our camping trip. It looks like it will rain again." Ashley looked out the window to a grey cloudy sky. She turned to the sound of footsteps and saw her mother standing in the doorway.

"I thought you had left."

"Not yet. I'll be staying with your grandmother a while in Aspen, Colorado so you know where I am going. After I've been there a month I'll go visit your father for a week."

"You're leaving me here all alone to deal with Sheryl missing? So you think I can handle it?"

"Yes, I'll be calling to check on you and you can call me if you need me. I don't think Sheryl would want us to sit around the house sulking and being upset all the time. I'm sure the police will do everything they can to help us." She could see the grimace on Ashley's face.

"It's like Sheryl vanished into thin air. When she comes home will you be very angry at her for not calling us. "No that would be too cruel dear, especially if it hadn't been her fault. We will help her to get her back on her feet again. I'll help her get a high school equivalency certificate. She would make a wonderful nurse I won't let anyone ruin her chances."

"I would like to question Greg Wager about her. Go have your fun. It's tempting to go with you. When do you leave?"

"In a few hours. Are you sure you should be playing police woman now?"

"Yes, Sheryl's got to be found," Ashley said with a smile.

"Well thank you for watching over Beth and this house. I wish you good luck while I'm gone. Make sure and call me, goodbye."

Ashley watched over Beth all week and gave her everything she needed. She loved all her little sisters and always wanted to give them whatever they wanted. She enjoyed watching Beth get better and knew soon her black hair, brown eyes, and pale skin would be tan again with pink cheeks and red lips that supported her smile.

The memory of Sheryl and her hazel eyes with brownish-red hair had been missing and lost somewhere. Still it kept coming back. It was very hard to forget. Ashley felt frustration like she had just lost her own child and wondered about Greg. Had this been his plan for revenge? Would he someday come back and kidnap Ashley's kid's years later? Beth's health did improve and she began eating more and more. Ashley had been expected to make sure Beth followed her mother's rules while she was gone but they didn't. They both wanted to have a fun wild time in their mother's house.

At first they weren't concerned if their mother ever came back. The problem with Sheryl missing was strong in their memories as they dealt with Beth's problem. They just wanted to feel happier.

"Let's invite Deanna over here so she doesn't have to stay alone. Immediately she got up to call Deanna, and ask her to come over to be with them. She ran back up to Beth's room and saw her getting back up out of bed trying to regain her strength. "When Deanna gets here we need to do something fun. We don't want it to be boring. Do you have the energy?"

"Yes, I think I will. What are we going to do?"

"I'm not sure so if you have any suggestions let me know. Pick somewhere it's my treat."

"Let's go to a comedy show. I've never been to one. Then do you want to go shopping at the mall with me?" Beth's sickness was obviously fading away to Ashley's delight, but she still had to finish her bottle of medication and take vitamins every day for a month, which were Ashley's own rules.

"Good idea Beth. How about we go tonight?"

"Fine," Beth said as she walked away into the bathroom.

"Deanna should be here soon then we'll go. I can't wait for you to meet her. I think you'll really like her."

Ashley and Deanna managed to make missing person posters of Sheryl with her picture on them and posted them at her job and handed some out to the local high school and all of the stores in a mall.

She stood in front of Sheryl's house looking to see if there was a way to get in. There is no sign of forced entry or break in. She did not have a house key and didn't see one under the doormat. Their aunt also lived there sometimes but wasn't there now. Ashley refused to believe that her aunt had been responsible for hurting Sheryl in any way.

Frustration began to come over Ashley because she wondered why the police weren't questioning Greg Wager or their aunt Pamela. Were the police really too busy? She felt this matter of Sheryl missing was going on too long. She felt she must do something herself.

Her first move would be to get inside Sheryl's house and look for clues that could tell her where she went and how she disappeared. There were two ways for her to get in the house. Either find Aunt Pamela's key or break a window and climb through it. She would have to find her aunt, but if that failed a window would have to get broken. Ashley intended on asking her mother where Aunt Pam went. For a moment the idea that her aunt may have also disappeared came to mind, but she refused to believe that. She wanted to believe her aunt was an airhead that had been out in some strange small town doing God knows what. One thing for sure, Pamela's job and Greg's house were her next destinations, but both those places were dangerous.

Ashley already had written a letter to Sheryl. It said:
Sheryl, call mom, me, Beth, or Tara when you get home. We are worried about you! Your sis, Ashley

She opened Sheryl's mailbox and found a stack of mail. She took it. She would call the post office and tell them to stop delivering. Ashley placed a flower on top of the envelope, got in her car, and drove away.

Getting back home she found Deanna. "What's going on with Greg's, I mean your money?"

"I don't want to fight him anymore. When I talked to him earlier he didn't want to give any money back. I think I can convince him to give me credit towards a new vacation. Where should I go?"

"I'll think about that. I'm not looking forward to looking

for Sheryl. I don't think my aunt will give me the key to Sheryl's house. When my mother comes back I'll ask her for it, or maybe she'll call. But I wish you luck and you can stay here as Long as you wish." They both were given a reason to smile.

Deanna entered the travel agency building smiling. She watched Greg Wager immediately glance up at her. The air felt clear and she felt she now had the chance to get her refund in a much easier way. "Greg, I'd like to use the credit I have coming toward a new vacation." She sat herself down at his desk and crossed her legs to look ladylike and polite in her dress.

The June heat dampened her body with sweat and a breeze blew her fragrant perfume through the air. She smelled nice.

"That depends. When and where would you like to go?"

"I want to go to British Columbia, Canada in August."

"I can give you credit to that trip if you do me a favor."

"What?"

"Cancel the court case and come over to my house tonight and have dinner with me?"

Deanna imagined the light of her victory and felt excited. Inside she didn't want to bother with a court case anymore.

"It's a deal." She put out her hand for him to shake. She was in the mood for forgiveness and thought Greg really isn't such a bad guy.

Greg wrote down his number and address on his business card and handed it to her. "Can you come over at six tonight?"

"I sure can. Thank you Greg. I look forward to seeing you tonight, bye."

Ashley looked at Deanna like she was crazy. "No way do I understand why you want to go to this dinner."

"It's easy. Greg will give me my vacation credit if I have a friendly dinner date with him."

"Alright take my cell phone and call me if something goes wrong."

"I'm sure it won't."

Chapter Five

Caleb and Greg rode back out to the country to see if
Sheryl's body was still there. When they saw that she was still
there they placed her in a bag and then in the trunk of the car
and took it home. "What are we going to do with the body?"
Greg asked.

"I don't know. Maybe bury it under our house. I don't
know what the right thing is to do. I'll bet her family's looking
for her."

"Deanna is coming over tonight for dinner so I can give her
credit for a vacation. Will you leave?"

"No I'm not leaving so you can prostitute her. I'll stay
upstairs. I didn't know you cooked. Do you?"

"Yes, it isn't that hard. I can make spaghetti fast or
whatever she wants. You know girls usually are impressed
when men cook them dinner."

"Is it a date?"

"Yes, I'm not that into her though."

"Let's just make sure sweet little Deanna doesn't run into
Sheryl tonight."

"I don't think she'll find her in the trunk, okay." Caleb
stepped harder on the gas pedal. Sheryl was left in the trunk of the car.
When Greg heard the sound of a car pull up in the driveway he thought it was
Deanna. It was. "Come in."
She dressed formally which showed she cared enough
about the date.

"Hi. Have a seat." Greg pointed to a tan leather chair.
Caleb was upstairs locked in a room and didn't plan on coming
out. Greg had no plans on telling Deanna Caleb was upstairs.

"Hi," she answered.

"How is spaghetti and wine for dinner?"

"That's fine."

"Then let's go to the dinner table, it's almost ready." Greg
took her arm and led her to a polished wooden table. Instead of
lighting romantic candles he had a lovely crystal chandelier
hanging above.

"So how are you feeling? Much better I hope, not
depressed?"

"No, I'm fine."

"Are you really interested in this date or are you here only
for vacation credit?"

"I'm here for both."

"My cousin called you a prostitute. I'll tell him he's
wrong. Would you like another date?"
Deanna was uncomfortable when he said that, but did not
have the courage to say no. "Yes sure I would." She was
uneasy.

"Okay we'll think about that idea soon and I'll call you
with a much more pleasant call next time. You can give me the
date and time when you want to leave for British Columbia and
I'll have your plane ticket for you."

"You know Sheryl, Ashley's little sister, is missing and I'm
staying with her to comfort her. She has this crazy idea you are
in some way responsible. Maybe she won't think you're the
enemy anymore."

Greg served spaghetti and poured wine.
Deanna began eating immediately. She watched Greg
thinking it was strange he didn't act offended about Ashley's
accusations. "Have you ever met Sheryl before?"

"No," Greg said as he sat down to eat. The crystal from the
chandelier reflected rainbow drops on her causing her to glow
with such beauty. For a moment he became attracted to her. It
was a shame she didn't feel the same way. "I'm sorry for the
trouble I caused you."

It was only a peace dinner to her. She ate quickly but Greg seemed to hesitate to tell her goodbye and let her go. It seemed to be over so soon. "Thanks for the lovely dinner." Deanna stood up. "I have to get back home now and thanks for your cooperation."

Greg took the plates into the kitchen. "Why don't you keep the rest of the bottle of wine I had been pouring and I'll call you tomorrow and we'll talk about another date." He handed her the bottle. They shook hands and she watched him walk her out the front door.

Deanna walked around to the front of the house and saw the large wooden gate to his back yard wide open. She wanted to do him a favor and close it so she stepped over to the backyard entry and looked in. It was a fairly large yard, but bare. No garden, grass, or chairs. She saw only one extremely large tree, a shed, and something covered over beside it. The wheel of a car showed.

"Greg has two cars. How glamorous. Maybe I should continue dating him." She lifted off the covering to see what he saved. Maybe he hid a convertible to take her on a romantic date to an expensive restaurant. She revealed a red station wagon that looked like her sister Sheryl's. The license plate was the same and the rip in the passenger seat was also in the same place. Deanna became convinced the car belonged to Sheryl.

Deanna took a deep breath of shock. What did this mean? Did he borrow the car from Sheryl? Had she stopped by to have him fix it? Did he steal it? One point became clear. She needed to know why Greg had the car while Sheryl had disappeared completely. Returning to the front door she knocked.

Greg opened it and said, "Yeah."

"Why do you have Sheryl Forester's car? Have you seen her?"

"Why don't you come in and have a seat." He opened the door wider.

Deanna stepped in and sat down.

"Sheryl came by here last week asking me about you, urging me to return your vacation money. She drove here and left her car here. I'm not sure why. That was just before she turned up missing. I heard about it when your court case got canceled. Maybe she's somewhere around here. Do you want me to help you look for her?"

"Sure, when?"

"Any time you want. I'm sure the sooner the better."

Caleb came down the steps holding a gun. He pointed it at Deanna. "Follow me."

They both began walking towards the basement.

"This isn't necessary," Greg informed Caleb. He followed them.

"We should put her in the attic," Caleb said.

"That's not going to be any better," Greg responded.

"Who cares? I don't want anyone to hear her scream."

They walked towards the basement. "Get in." Caleb left the room.

"It's only for a little while. I'll let you out tomorrow. Goodnight, I'll see you in the sunlight." He shut the door and closed the lock behind him.

The basement had been made to look like a comfortable room with a couch, rugs, and chairs. Deanna did not feel tired but cried and shut the light off. She sensed trouble for her and for Sheryl. Something didn't seem right in Victorville. She closed her eyes to try to get some sleep. The sooner the day ended the better. The quicker she fell asleep the faster she would wake up to the morning.

Deanna woke at two in the morning to sounds coming from the house. The walls were thin enough to allow the sounds in.

Laying in the dark she could hear loud voices and banging doors that slammed. She heard Caleb's voice. "We're doing this now because it's the best time!"

She then heard Greg's voice. "Then this time we'll have to dump Sheryl somewhere more obvious."

Deanna took a deep breath. "I can't believe it," she whispered. "Sounds like Sheryl's dead or injured and they have her." She wanted to assume it had been their fault. The idea of dating Greg again had become disgusting. She also wanted to call Ashley on her cell phone, but it would have to wait until daylight.

For the next two hours Deanna couldn't sleep. All she wanted to do was grieve for poor Sheryl. It was awful that a nice person like Sheryl died, or maybe she was just hurt. Could she really believe what she heard? She had to know. There was only one window, but if she broke it they might hear it. She sat closer to the wall.

"We can dump her in a neighborhood park. It's the only one that is ten minutes from here. This nightmare turned real will soon be all over with," Caleb said. "See it's okay. We didn't mean to kill her. I just wanted to defend you and I whacked her in the back of her head. Shit she had a gun. We can call it self defense."

"What about Deanna Jennings?" Greg asked.

"Leave her down there. No, I don't care what you do with her."

Deanna woke to sunlight. Minutes then hours seemed to slip by and no one came. Unable to wait any longer Deanna began to pound on the door as hard as she could yelling, "Greg get down here! If you don't get down here I'll kick the door down."

Finally the door opened and he came in.

"Let me go."

He didn't move.

"I know you did something to Sheryl, so let me out of here, please."

"You can't leave yet."

"Is it because I suspect you guys did something to Sheryl?"

"Yes."

"How long did you have her? When and how did she die? Just tell me instead of making things complicated with a long tough investigation."

Greg sat down on the brown couch. He was sobbing.

"Sheryl died the day Ashley and you left to go on vacation. She came here by her own free will. I swear to you she had a gun and pointed it at me in this house. Caleb became frightened and hit her on the back of the head with something. She fell unconscious and never woke up again. So you see she almost died of natural causes. We left her near a pond for the police to find but they didn't find her after one night. That night there had been a storm and when we came back to check out the scene Sheryl's lifeless face was submerged in water from the night's rain. We put her in our trunk and now we still have her. I didn't feel like anyone would find her at that point. We took her dead body to a park down the road last night. I'm sorry about all this. If you tell anyone we will deny everything." Greg looked up. Deanna was gone. She had run out of the room while he was wiping his teary eyes.

He ran out to the front yard and her car was gone. She had driven away quickly. Driving 75 miles an hour towards the park Deanna had been hoping the police had already found Sheryl's body, or that she was still alive. She stopped in the parking lot and ran out of the car. She ran all over the area, calling Sheryl's name. Sheryl's body couldn't be found anywhere. A block away was a grocery store and she stopped and called Ashley.

"Ashley's not here," Beth said on the other line.

"Can you please tell her Deanna Jennings called?"

"Okay, my sister should be back in an hour."

"Thanks, bye."
Hanging up the phone she thought she saw a hand laying
on the ground behind a bush. Running over to the area she saw
it was Sheryl. She screamed and sat down on the ground
holding Sheryl's hand for a time. Deanna then called the
police. "The body is Sheryl Forester. She lived on 400 Brown
drive in Victorville, California. Her sisters are Beth, Tara, and
Ashley. They live nearby and so does her mother," She told
them.

"We'll be out there in a few minutes," the lady on the
phone replied.

Deep inside Deanna wanted to run far away but stayed by
to wait for the police to show up. Shortly they did and Deanna
stayed to watch them cover her up, take pictures, then take her
away." The question now was; how would Ashley find out?
Should Deanna go back to Ashley's house? Would Ashley
blame Deanna? They were best friends but Deanna had to
wonder about how long that might last. She also wondered if
Ashley would become depressed.

Deanna went back to Ashley's home. She really didn't
want to be responsible for telling Ashley the bad news. When
she arrived home Ashley was not there. Neither was Beth.
The house was still and quiet, like death. "I wonder what
happened to them."

As Deanna passed through the kitchen she saw a message
on their answering machine. She felt afraid to listen because
Ashley might mind. Evening fell on the house. The house
darkened a little more and still no one had come home. She
began to be anxious and didn't feel like doing anything. A
wave of worry came over her and she picked up the kitchen
phone to call Tara. When Tara didn't answer she dialed
Ashley's cell phone.
"Is everything okay? How come you aren't home?"
Deanna asked when Ashley answered the phone.

"No, Beth is in the hospital. She's sick. The doctors think
it might be cancer."

"When are you coming home?"

"I'm at the hospital now and I'll probably be here all night."

"Okay." Deanna did not have the guts to tell Ashley more bad news, so she tried to let her know carefully. "Will you call the police? They have information on Sheryl's disappearance. It's important. Please don't worry. We'll get through these times together. I'll make dinner and clean the house and wait for you in the morning. Do you think Beth will be okay?"

"I'm not sure. She's so sick she can't even stand. I can't believe this; I thought she was getting better. I'm calling my mother after I call the police. Goodnight Dean."

By morning when Deanna woke up she called, "Ashley!" When there was no answer she ran around the house and looked out the window for Ashley's car. No one answered and she felt Ashley didn't come home because she had found out about Sheryl. Deanna decided she had to run over to the local hospital and find Beth and hopefully Ashley would be there too. She wanted more than anything to comfort Ashley at this time. She would be her best friend and be at her side all week without working on her job for two weeks.

Deanna arrived at the hospital quickly. "I'm looking for Beth Forester. What room is she in?"

The receptionist replied, "Oh." and began looking through a computer for the room. "She's in room 256. I'm sure she's awake now so go ahead and drop in for a little while. It's on the second floor at the second door on the left."

"Thanks," Deanna immediately went to the elevator. She found Beth sitting up looking pale and watching TV. "Hi Beth, I'm Deanna Jennings. I called you before. I'm Ashley's roommate. How are you?"

"Not good. I'm very sick. I think it's the medication. Ashley's down on the first floor at the gift shop. We heard the bad news about Sheryl. She's dead. She's down at the morgue getting an autopsy and her funeral is in a week. The police think it was a freak accident, but they're making sure a murder has not been committed."

"Right; how is Ashley taking it?"

"She misses Sheryl. It's hard to let go sometimes. She never spoke much to me though. I think Ashley's going to be okay. I just hope I will be too. I don't want to be buried next to Sheryl soon. My mother is coming back from Colorado tomorrow. You can stay here with me. You know they actually have good food here. Ashley will be back soon."

"Okay." Deanna sat down in a chair. "Are you going to be strong enough to make it to the funeral?"

"I don't know, but I'm going anyway. My mother will probably roll me in a wheel chair."

Ashley appeared in the room. She suddenly didn't seem so intimidating any more. "Hi, Deanna Sheryl's dead and Beth might have cancer. How could this happen?"

"You'll make it though won't you Beth," asked Deanna. Beth smiled and nodded.

"Let's go home," Ashley suggested. They just went home to grieve.

Beth spent the remaining week waiting for her surgery, which would take place several days before Sheryl's funeral. She spent the time mostly in bed being quiet without the strength to do much. The day of the surgery Beth had been put to sleep and the next thing she remembers is dreaming. She dreamed about sleeping on water and fish swimming around her. Then she wandered on a tropical island. She had many paradise dreams until finally the next morning she woke feeling rejuvenated and better. The place where the skin cancer had been on her scalp felt bare and empty now that it was gone she was sure she would be alright. A large grin came to her face but went away at the thought of what she would wear to the funeral the day after tomorrow.

After drinking plenty of juice and putting on her best black dress Beth's mother Darlene came to pick her up for the funeral. To Beth's surprise she saw her sisters Tara and Ashley with her.

"Get your suitcase. Don't you want to go home after the funeral? We will all be at my house. Even Deanna and Tara's friend Kenny will be there."

Beth nodded. "I'm sick of staring at these walls." She took her purse and placed her medicine bottle in it and Darlene took her suitcase.

Tara had been the only sister intending on staying at her mother's six-bedroom two level house for only a week. She wanted to get back to Kenny's house. He was her roommate and immediately Beth wondered if Tara had a crush on him. The funeral seemed slightly short. It lasted less than an hour. After placing flowers on Sheryl's gravestone they all prayed then it was over. Goodbye to Sheryl didn't seem to last long enough and soon the priest left the area. They all planned to visit her grave at least once a week with prayers, candles, plants and flowers.

Darlene didn't say much that night. She was completely quiet. She missed her daughter's face. Sheryl had been so pretty to her. The first impression by the police had been that Sheryl drowned but they didn't know how her teenage face had ended up face down in a puddle.

Frustration filled Darlene. Her divorce, her job, and now her youngest had died. Each one of her daughters had their own room in that house but Sheryl was not there. Darlene seemed glad Deanna had been staying with them but Ashley could only give her Sheryl's old room. Deanna did not want to take it and she just slept on the couch and sometimes Ashley's floor. Deanna didn't mind. She loved the Forester sisters as if they were her own family. Sheryl's room looked like a tomb with framed pictures of her with candles and flowers and goodbye notes from the family.

"Did you tell the police Greg Wager is responsible for Sheryl's death?" Ashley asked Deanna.

"I didn't. I met his cousin Caleb and they gave me a hard time the night I had dinner there. That's why I didn't come home that night. He gives me the creeps too. I should have told the police what happened. Greg told me he would deny everything if I told anyone and I was afraid of him. How will we prove it now?"

"Alright, I'll tell the police and my mother will help us."

"What do you think of torturing Greg into a confession?" Deanna gave out a small snicker.

"Sounds interesting, he probably deserves it," Ashley answered.

"Greg and Caleb both do."

"Maybe you could convince Greg into confessing to the police by having another date with him. We'll think of a strategy and you can get fixed up all sexy and pretty to tempt him."

"Yes, that's a good idea." Deanna's face lit up. She liked the idea.

"I'll have your back. I took karate when I was a kid and I was a brown belt but I'm still pretty good. I think I can take him. Maybe we could hire you a body guard."

"I'll think about that one, but one thing's for sure. The evil cousins must be stopped before they hurt someone else and I'm up to all sorts of ideas Ashley."

"I want to hear them scream they're sorry. How do you think Sheryl ended up face down in the water?"

"Greg and Caleb, they killed her."

"Could it have been a suicide?"

"No, the police don't think so either and they didn't find a suicide note.

"The autopsy report says nothing about alcohol or drugs in Sheryl's blood. They did find water in Sheryl's lungs though. I feel like I should have been watching her. I feel bad." Ashley's frown was hidden when she bowed her head to the ground. The longer Sheryl had been gone the more Ashley missed and loved her sister. Deanna became sure what she wanted to do at that point. She didn't want to see Greg but knew they didn't have any evidence. "I'll take a small tape recorder to record his confession." She knew Greg and Caleb were responsible for Sheryl's death and Ashley had been the only other person who believed the story. "I'm sure Greg will be asking soon for another date. I just hope this works."

Chapter Six

"I'm going over to Greg's house this Sunday," Deanna announced to Ashley.

"We'll think of a way to make sure you're safe. We'll come up with a strategy." Ashley sat down next to Deanna.

"Sunday is in two days. I'll follow you to Greg's house and make sure you come out in a certain amount of time."

"Of course her car is probably still in his back yard. Do you want me to ask for it back?"

"We'll ask for it after we report it to the police. I'll call them right now." Ashley got up to dial the phone.

"On Sunday I'll bring a small tape recorder to put in my pocket." Deanna quieted down as she watched Ashley listen on the phone. "These guys are so caught." Ashley continued with her report on the phone. She would talk and it seemed the police would just follow her words.

"Good news. They're going over today to look at the car today."
The police did not call back until the evening. "The police are on the phone and they want to keep the car and check it over for DNA.

"Are they talking about arresting Greg and Caleb?" Deanna asked back.

"Yes, they might if they get some more evidence. They seem to think Sheryl's death had been an accident but they want to investigate more. Until they figure it out Greg and Caleb are free."

"Then yes. I'm still going to have a talk with Greg and I want you to go in with me. We will do it this Sunday."

"I just don't want to say anything that will make Greg want to run away. I don't want him to hurt anyone again. We won't tell him the police are watching him."

"Okay, I'll go with you," Ashley agreed.

"What ever happened to your aunt Pamela?" Deanna asked.

"I don't know. Maybe she left for Europe. Maybe she was afraid we would accuse her of something.

"I can't stand the idea of seeing Greg again, but I'll do it for Sheryl to get justice for her. I'm going to call him now and tell him I'm coming to visit him on Sunday. I won't tell him about the police checking Sheryl's car."

Deanna went to speak with Greg on Sunday. Deanna was nearby.

"If you want to clear you conscience you'll have to go to the local police station and tell them what happened with Sheryl. Cooperate with everything they want. Understand what I'm saying, it's about justice for Sheryl so she and all of us can rest in peace."

"That makes no sense honey. They've figured out how she died in the autopsy, it was an accident, and that's all the justice she needs. It's not like someone raped her then shot her in the head. You should relax and get some rest. You're upset because Sheryl has just recently died. I'm upset too. We don't have to see one another for a while until you feel better. I promise I didn't kill Sheryl on purpose and I'm sorry for the way I treated you when I locked you in that room. Don't be afraid. I'll try to make it up to you on our next date so forget the idea of me going to jail because I don't think it's going to happen."

"I can't stand the thought of dating you again." A sudden knock at the door caught Deanna's attention.
Greg answered the door. "Is Deanna here? Can I see her?"
Deanna went to the door. "I'm doing okay." She turns to Greg. "I've heard your side of this situation and we're not going out on a date until you tell the police what happened. She held her crossed fingers behind her back.

"Promise me you will never behave that way again." She watched Greg nod as they walked out the door holding her breath.

"Okay, I'll promise. When do you think the police will arrest me?" Greg asked.

"I'm not sure but I want you to be here when they come and I want you to tell them the truth." Greg watched her leave as he wondered what he would do. Should he stay or run? He knew running would only leave him wanted by the law and without Deanna. At that moment he realized his only choice was to stay and deal with situation. He didn't want to leave and run from the police without Deanna. He wanted to stay and go on seeing her. He wanted to fall in love with her. He hoped Caleb would take all the blame. He felt Caleb should have taken it. It must have been his fault.

Greg realized at that moment Caleb hadn't been home. He wondered if Caleb would ever come home. Was he hiding from the law? Greg sat on a chair. "It's a deal Deanna my dear. I'll explain everything to the police. It had been Caleb's fault any way. I'll do that and then expect to hear from me soon. I'd like to take you on a nice date. We'll go to the ballet or something. Whatever you like we'll do. I'm going to stay home and hope and wait for Caleb to come home. I promise you."

Deanna smiled and said, "Okay," as she went to the car. Greg lay on his couch waiting for Caleb. As the minutes went by he didn't know when Caleb would come home. As he listened to the kitchen sink drip he sat up to look around the house for a note. When he didn't find anything he went into Caleb's room to look. Nothing appeared in the room that left a clue. Pulling open the closet door he saw half of Caleb's clothes were missing. It was a sign that Caleb had left to stay somewhere else. How did he know Deanna called the police? Greg wondered if he had heard Deanna talking about it. Greg's first idea was to look for Caleb. "If I had been Caleb where would I go?" Greg asked himself. He didn't know where Caleb would be. One of the best ideas he had would be to ask Caleb's boss where he could have gone.

"Thanks for saying goodbye." Another reason Greg felt glad Caleb had left had been he could invite Deanna over and they could be alone. Greg had to decide if he would tell the police where Caleb had gone. After growing up with his cousin he thought he might be able to find him, but a part of him did not want to turn him in. "I can't wait until this is over." Greg crossed his fingers the police would never come.

Greg slept comfortably and felt safe when loud bangs were heard in his dreams. He jumped up. He heard the sound of knocking on the door. He got up and quickly combed his hair then went to the door. Looking out the peek hole he felt surprised at what he saw. There were several police officers standing there. Greg opened the door.

"Greg Wager, we need to have a talk about Sheryl Forester. I saw that you have her car parked in your backyard," the officer stated.

"That's right. She left it here a couple weeks ago I think."

"Her sisters would like Sheryl's car back. We are going to check it out first here's the warrant for us to come onto your property. Let's talk about how the girl died. The autopsy shows she drowned I just need to make sure someone didn't assist her in that. The only suspects we have are you and your cousin Caleb. Where is your cousin?"

"I don't know, but I'm going to look for him."

"Are you really? Well, how about if I take you down to the police station and we'll talk about this situation with a tape recorder on the table. We can help you look for him. Let's go."

Greg put his wallet in his pocket, took his keys, and went out the door with the officer. The officer opened the police car door and Greg got in.

"I'm Officer Norman by the way."

"I swear I didn't know Sheryl would die," Greg pleaded.

"Save it for when we get to the station."

A few moments later they were at the local police station.

"Don't worry the gate was open and for the car to be towed." The officer acted like he was impressed by Greg's cooperation. They both went in and sat down at a desk. The officer pulled out some papers and Greg saw the name Sheryl Forester at the top. "I'll ask you before a judge asks you." Greg saw Mr. Norman push turn on his tape recorder. "Did you deliberately drown Sheryl Forester?"

"No, well she came by to ask me to refund Deanna Jennings some money and I couldn't but she came into the house. She seemed a little reckless because she had a gun in her purse and pulled it out. I had called the police a while ago to have them come get it but they never did and Caleb came and took it." Greg was lying to the officer.

"How did he get it?" asked Officer Norman.

"Sheryl passed out. I don't think she had the nerve to shoot me. We took her gun and assuming she would be okay and someone would find her we took her out to a local field near the highway and dropped her off. We thought she would catch a ride from someone. We didn't know it would rain. I know my cousin can be a little rough but I don't think he could have known Sheryl would die. If that had been how she died. I've also taken care of my problem of a refund with Deanna.

"I don't know why I should believe you. You know lying to an officer about a possible crime is serious, don't you?"

"Yes sir," Greg replied.

"Well then I choose to believe you because there's no way we can prove you murdered Sheryl at this time. But where the heck is your cousin Caleb Wager?" Officer Norman asked I want to question him also.

"I don't know."

"Why don't you call his work and ask about him. You can use our phone. You two could be charged with her death it's up to the DA. Is that the reason your cousin won't come in and talk to us?"

Greg pulled the phone towards himself. "I don't know." He picked it up to call Caleb's manager. Caleb worked for a construction company.

"Hi, can I speak to the manager?"
Mr. Norman could hear that phrase coming from Greg.

"Have you seen Caleb Wager? Did he transfer
somewhere? Is he? Can I talk to him? Okay, bye."

"Caleb is working right now. I don't know where he was
last night. I couldn't talk to him."

"After lunch I'm going to take you back home and I want
you to stay there until I call you in a week or less to tell you
what's going on. I can't promise that you won't get arrested."

Greg left the office to walk to a restaurant to eat. He found
a pay phone and called Deanna. "I'm by the police station.
They are thinking about charging us with negligence or maybe
involuntary manslaughter. I kept my part of the bargain now I
want to pick you up tomorrow night? I told Officer Norman
everything you wanted."

"Okay now I have to keep my end of the bargain."

"I'll pick you up at five in the evening. How's that?"

"That's fine."

Deanna knew she would have to continue seeing Greg as long
as he wanted. She didn't want him to take off before he was
arrested for the murder of Sheryl

"Okay. Do you still want to go to Canada? I think I want
to go with you."

"Yes I'll go. Are you serious?"

"It's probably just an idea. I'm sorry about all this, really.
I didn't mean to hurt anyone. I want to grieve for Sheryl too.
You should have seen her the last time I saw her. She had a
gun pointed right at me, the poor thing. I'll call you tomorrow
before I pick you up okay? Bye."

When Greg awoke in the morning the first thing he wanted
to do was call Deanna. He decided it could wait until after
breakfast and when he passed through the hall he felt surprised

to see Caleb sleeping in his bed. Greg looked through the door at him. "We can't leave here Caleb," Greg whispered. "I think everything will be okay."

Caleb rolled over and looked at Greg. He woke him up with his whispering.

"Caleb, where do you think I should take Deanna out on a date?"

"Don't you think you should ask her?" Caleb asked.

"Yes, you're right. I'll ask when I call her."
Caleb fell back asleep.

Immediately Greg went to the phone to call Deanna. She isn't home so he calls Ashley's house. "I figured you would be there."

"I'm living here now. Didn't you know that? I'm moving the rest of my furniture and selling my old house. Ashley and I are going to be roommates now."

"Where are we going tonight?" Greg asks Ashley.

"There's this new musical I'm dying to see. I think it's called a Broadway Review. It's playing at the local playhouse. Can we go see it?"

"Of course. What time?"

"How about tonight at six? Could we go then?"

"Definitely," Greg answered. "Before I pick you up I'm going to stop by Travel World agency and get you your ticket to go to British Columbia in August. Do you want to stay at the Hilton hotel?"

"Yes."

"I'll make your reservations today. You want to leave August 8th and come back on the twenty second right?" Greg asked.

"Yes. So have you done any interesting traveling yourself lately?" Deanna asked.

"I've been many places and since I get discounts I like to vacation at least once a year."

"Just try not to accidentally take a vacation to Mexico if the police decide you're going to jail."

"I've been to Mexico but not every state and country. Who the hell has been to every country and state? I don't know. I told you that I'm really sorry about Sheryl Forester. Did you know her well?"

"No, Ashley's my best friend and I only saw Sheryl a few times. It's scary though you know, being close to someone who is missing. I'm also the person who found her body."

"Well I'm sorry. I don't have a good education. I didn't graduate the eighth grade and I didn't know Sheryl would die, I swear. I wish she was still alive. The last time I saw her she was mad at me holding a gun with a purse around her shoulder. I liked her but she may have hated me. And it had been all for you. I would think you guys were better friends; she was trying to get your money back from me.

"Maybe sometime we could go to Mexico together. It seems so foreign to me and so romantic." Greg was hoping she was falling for his line.

"I don't think so Ashley and I are planning to go New Mexico."

"Okay, I'll pick you up in a few hours."

A knock could be heard echoing through the Forester house. Ashley looked out the front window and saw grey clouds covering the summer July sky. She also saw Greg Wager. "Great, Mr. wonderful is here. Deanna, I think it's for you!"

Deanna straightened out her small dresser she had just moved from her old house when she heard Ashley call. "I'm coming." Deanna put on her black heels and her black purse around her shoulder and opened the front door. "Hi."

"Did you want to get ready before we go, though we need
to leave in a few minutes?" Greg asked.

"Very funny, I think you know I'm already ready. Let's
go. I want to get a good seat."

Greg smiled at Deanna, he thought he was funny.
Riding in Greg's car Deanna watched Greg every few
seconds.

"Why did you bring your purse? You know I'm paying."
After Deanna nodded he asked, "What is that old large house
like? Is it creepy at night with strange sounds?"

"I was already nervous with Sheryl missing. Did you know
Beth is sick? It's probably cancer. But I think I love the house
and the Forester family. I want to see the huge mansion Tara
Forester lives in with that guy. It's so big it looks mysterious."

"I could take you to see it. Do you think Tara would let us
in?" Greg asked.

"I don't know. I think it's over on Pine road. I like stuff
out in the country." Deanna watched him pull into the parking
lot of the theatre.

Once they got in they both sat down close to the front.

"Here are your tickets." Greg handed her the plane tickets.
"The hotel has your reservations. When do you want to go to Tara's?" he
asked.

"I have to call her and ask if it's alright," she told him.

"Have you seen Sheryl's ghost yet?" Greg asked. He had a
sick sense of humor.

"No, but I haven't been up in her room at night yet. There's something I
want to tell you and I don't know if you'll see it as good or bad news."

"What you saw Sheryl's ghost and you were just afraid to tell me?"

"No."

"Someone else's ghost?"

"No. In September Ashley and I are moving to New Mexico. In fact I don't think I'll be unpacking all of my stuff. When I get there I'll start studying to become a social worker. I've already have most of my education finished and I'll try to find an internship." She told Greg this because she couldn't stand the thought of him asking her out again.

Greg didn't take this as good news. He rolled his eyes.

"We should also go on a farewell date but I have to be honest. I don't want you to go." Everyone stopped talking and a spotlight came on the stage. The audience clapped for the first singers.

The next day Deanna woke up a little stiff and tired from the night before. Watching musicals always made her more tired. They usually went on for several hours. Looking at her answering machine she saw there had been a message. She got up and pushed play.

"Deanna Jennings, it's me Greg Wager. Can you call me back bye?" Deanna picked up the phone and called him."

"Greg, let me guess. You want to go on a date to Tara's? I haven't even called my sister yet. Why don't we wait a few days? We just went out yesterday. Just let me call Tara, and then I'll call you back. Ashley wants me to help her pack some of her stuff. In a couple days she's going to New Mexico to put a down payment on our house and check out the town and her new work place as a vet's assistant." Greg seemed agreeable and Deanna called Tara. She found they could go to Tara's whenever they want. She was desperately hoping this was the last time she would have to see Greg.

"We could ride up there and it can be a sort of date. We could leave now then stay in a motel. It only takes an hour to get there." Greg was hoping she would agree.

Deanna did agree and packed her bags. Greg pulled up in his

car.

"Just one minute," Deanna said as she ran back to the house.

"Ashley I'm leaving. I'm going to visit Tara. Greg and I will be staying in that town a couple nights. We get to see the house she now lives in. I wanted to say goodbye to you since we're both traveling at the same time."

"Do you really trust that Greg?" Ashley asked.

"No, but I have to keep him here so he doesn't run away. He's just a sorry companion."

"Okay, bye then. If you need to you can call Tara or my mother for help."

Deanna walked away out the door to leave for Tara's house.

Chapter Seven

Deanna and Greg pulled up to the house. There wasn't any driveway so they only parked in some grass. "I love big houses," Deanna pointed out. The house seemed spooky on the outside. It looked very large with many windows.

Deanna approached the front door and knocked as hard as she could. Tara answered. "Hi sorry I knocked so hard it was my first reaction. It seems so big I wanted to make sure you heard me."

Tara smiled. "Hi." She opened the door wider and Deanna could see the inside of the house looked cozy and beautifully decorated. "Come in."

They both stepped in. "Great house," Deanna said smiling. "Is it haunted?"

"I don't know. We can ask Kenny when he gets home. I don't know when that is. This house is so large. Why don't you spend the night?"

"I'm sure we'd love to but we already paid for our rooms," Deanna answered.

"Can't you get your money back?" Tara asked.

"Maybe we can. I'm not sure."

"I can get you something to drink. After I bring you your drinks you can explore the whole house. I still think you should spend the night."

"Okay, that sounds like a good idea," Greg responded. "I'll go get our money back just for tonight Deanna. I'll be back soon."

Deanna didn't really want to be left alone but had no choice. What did Ashley mean? Could Greg be trusted? The situation was starting to give Deanna a very bad feeling. She didn't say anything so no one would be insulted and get defensive.

While holding her ice tea Deanna walked up to the second floor. Darkness started to fall over the house. Looking out a front window she saw Greg was just leaving. "Damn him I hate him."

"Who?" A man asked.

Deanna heard a man's voice and it frightened her. She turned around. "Who are you?"

"Kenny Walker." He must have come home.

"Where's Tara?" she asked.

"When you can't find anyone around this house you should go to the front door and ring the door bell. That gets Tara's attention every time. Trust me, I've used it myself."

"Okay," Deanna smiled. He seemed likeable.

"She should be in our bedroom. I'll take you there." He started walking down a hall and she followed him.

"Are you Tara's boyfriend?" Deanna asked.

"Yes I very much am. She is so beautiful."

"When Tara talks about you to her sisters she says the same thing about you."

"Is Greg your boyfriend?" he asked.

"No." Deanna followed him into the room and saw Tara sitting on the bed.

"Where is your boyfriend?" Tara looked frustrated.

"He's not my boyfriend, but I'm sure he will be back any minute." The doorbell rang. "I'll bet that's him." Deanna followed them out to get the door. When they opened it there he stood. "Taking your time I see."

Greg entered the house with two bags of clothes. He

watched Tara and Kenny walk away.

"What room are we sleeping in?" Greg asked.

Deanna turned to Greg. "It's not room it's rooms. I'll ask
her which room you're sleeping in. Where the heck did she
go? Let's go into the living room."

Greg nodded and they went to the living room to sit.

Tara followed them into the room. "You can sleep in any
upstairs bedrooms you want."

It started getting darker and Deanna felt tired, she nodded
and they both went upstairs to pick their rooms. They saw only
one room that had a large bed. All the others had old furniture
everywhere but no big beds. "Looks like this is it," Deanna
said.

They both sat down. They saw the room didn't have a
couch only one chair and a bookcase. Wind blew in through
the window and Deanna closed it.

"Do you like this house?" Greg asked.

"Yes, it's big," she answered. "Who gets the bed?"

"We both do," Greg answered.

"I don't think so."

"Then what will we do?" Greg asked.

"I don't know. Do you like sleeping on floors?" Deanna
asked.

"Yes but I want to sleep on the bed."

"That means I'm getting on the floor. Maybe I can sleep in
the chair. But I don't have an extra blanket." Deanna
continued to sit on the bed.

The house had become quiet and it seemed like Tara and

Kenny had gone to sleep. Greg turned out the lights and Deanna laid there in the dark. She felt glad she hadn't been alone but didn't want to be sleeping next to Greg.

Deanna woke to the sound of birds chirping. She figured Greg must have opened it but she couldn't find him in the room. Quickly Deanna got up and looked to see if his car could be seen out front and it was. Deanna combed her hair then left the room to look for him.

Greg stood near the end of the stairs. "Deanna we're leaving now." He ran up the stairs and took their bags. "We'll stop and get something to eat on the way home."

"I want to say goodbye to Tara." Deanna ran over to Tara's room. "We're leaving now. Thank you for having us."

"Okay bye, you can go into the kitchen and have something to eat if you want."

"Alright we will." Deanna walked away to the kitchen. When she got there she opened the refrigerator and took a bagel.

"What are you doing?" Greg asked.

"What does it look like?"

"Let's go, now."

Deanna put her juice and bagel back and they went out the front door to leave.

While riding in the car Greg asked her, "Are you still moving?"

"Yes," Deanna answered.

"Then we should have one last date this weekend. Think about where you want to go and you can tell me when I pick you up this weekend. We can go to church, or to the movies, or to a concert, anything."

"That's fine. Just one last date," Deanna answered.
Deanna entered the Forester home she now lived in. She

ran into Ashley in the hallway.

"I wish you'd stop seeing Greg Wager. I'm starting to pack my belongings. Why don't you start packing yours," Ashley suggested then she went on her way.

Deanna kept her furniture in storage in the backyard shed because she had moved all her furniture out of her house. She entered her bedroom that was on the other side of the house from Beth Forester and two rooms down from Ashley's.

Ashley entered the room. "I kind of don't want to move. I think I'll really miss Beth. Oh well I've got a good idea. What do you think if we both go down to New Mexico tomorrow and look for a house together?"

"That's a great idea. I'd love to."

"Alright, we'll get up early and go. How's that?" Ashley asked.

"Okay good." Deanna began packing for the trip. "How long do you think we'll be there?"

"I don't know. As long as we need to be."

"Okay I can call Greg and we'll go on our farewell date when we get back."

"How can you stand him?" Ashley asked.

"I'm stringing him along so I can keep my eyes on him. I just get a little afraid of him at times."

"Well we are moving away. What town would you like to live in? My job is in Albuquerque."

"I don't mind. Do you think we could actually go to Mexico? I've never been there and I'd love to go. I love Mexican food, and Chinese food."

"Of course that would be a great idea. I promise you we'll go some time."

"I need to be back from New Mexico by August though because I have my tickets to go to British Columbia."

"That's fine. I don't think it will be longer than a week. I'm going to work as a veterinarian's assistant and train to be a vet. What do you want to do?"

"I want to be a social worker. If there's a school near by I'd like to study as soon as we get there." When Ashley left the room Deanna laid down to start resting.

Deanna woke the next morning to Ashley shaking her.

"Get up. I've got a good idea. Let's bring Beth."

Ashley nodded. In an hour the car had been loaded with luggage and they were ready to leave. "In about four hours we'll be in Arizona. Then we can stop," Ashley said as they drove down the highway.

It happened as Ashley said and by the next night they were in Santa Fe, New Mexico. The motel sat in a desert looking area. There were lizards and cactus. The sun felt very hot.

They were sweating as Ashley and Beth went in to get a room. There didn't seem to be much else in the area but horses and dirt. Deanna felt glad she had worn her sandals and dress. She picked up her suitcase and went in.

Beth and Ashley shared a room but Deanna had her own. She laid her suitcase down on the blue carpet and collapsed on the bed. She heard a knock on the door.

"Deanna!" The voice belonged to Ashley and Deanna answered it. "Why don't you rest and tomorrow we'll go looking around and you can look for a job."

"Okay. I want to be a social worker. I'll check out the school," Deanna answered.

"The day after that we'll go looking at houses for sale. Do you like it here?" Ashley asked.

"Yes, I love it. I can't wait to stay. It seems so peaceful."

"We don't have much money but I'm sure we can find an old cozy house. Wouldn't it be fun to live in a house that had been built in the 1800's? I'll be looking in the newspaper for houses for sale. Why don't you look too?"

"Okay," Deanna smiled at Ashley as she left the room to go to her own.

It still looked dark out at five in the morning when Deanna woke. The room appeared black but Deanna could hear sobs coming from down the hallway. She could then recognize the sound of Ashley's voice talking but she couldn't understand it.

Then she heard a knock at the door and assumed it was Ashley.

"Beth has a cold. I want her to rest by herself, especially without spreading her germs to me. Can I stay here with you?" Ashley asked.

"Of course."
Ashley entered the room. "I don't think we should have brought her. I think she's having a relapse. Damn, I thought it would be a good idea. Where should I sleep?"

"You can have the bed; I'll fix a spot on the couch."

"Okay, I'll go and get my sheets. I'll probably be taking Beth to the doctor tomorrow. I may have to spend some time with her so I'll drop you off at the mall."

Deanna woke in the morning light to find Ashley gone. There appeared to be a note on the table. Deanna took it and read it.

Dear Deanna, I've gone to take Beth to the hospital. I'll be back at 1 o'clock to take you to the school, and then I have to get back to the hospital again. Luv, Ashley

She looked at the clock and it said twelve thirty. She jumped up to hurry and get ready to go. While Deanna took a shower she heard a knock at the door. She answered the door after covering up. Ashley entered the room.

"Beth has had a relapse. I think she'll be in the hospital

until we leave," Ashley said. "I grabbed the local newspaper and read the classifieds. There are a few inexpensive houses we can check out in this area."

"I'll be ready in a few minutes." Deanna got dressed then put hair in a ponytail and took her purse with her.
On the way to the school to pick up registration forms Ashley asked, "Do you want to come with me back to the hospital? We'll just be there to bring her something to eat and keep her company for a while."

"Yes I do. It's better than sitting around the room. I'd like to see Beth and bring her flowers. Let's get some."

The school in town looked small and brown on the outside with the inside decorated very colorful like the motel. They looked at it together. "I'll bet there are lots of cute guys here,"

Deanna said. "I want to get this done quickly, even if I have to take classes online."

"Okay we've seen it. Let's go," Ashley said.

They both entered Beth's room with a half dozen red roses.

Beth appeared pale.

"I don't feel so good. Will you guys come back and get me tomorrow to visit after you look at homes?" Beth asked.

"Of course we'll be here every day until it's time to go home," Ashley answered.

A nurse entered the room and Beth closed her eyes. "Beth, Beth?" the nurse called. "She must be falling asleep. She's been ill for a while hasn't she? Now it's not so simple. Her cancer has complications. The doctor will be in to talk to you soon. She's your sister isn't she? The bad news is you probably won't be able to take her back home with you to California. I'm sorry. I'll send the doctor in here soon."

"Beth, do you want us to bring you a magazine to read?" Ashley asked.

Beth nodded yes. "Anything, as long as it's interesting. I trust your judgment."

"And guess what? I'm bringing you soup for dinner in a minute," Ashley said. "And don't worry Beth you'll be alright. You'll be alright. You're so young we're sure you can fight it."

After those things were given to Beth they watched TV together until Beth fell asleep and it became evening. Ashley turned off the TV and the lights and they left shutting the door behind them.

Back at the motel they both sat at a public table beside a warm fireplace. Deanna had tears in her eyes. The trip had now become a time of mourning. "I can't believe it. I might lose two sisters in the same year." Ashley said noticing the sky had become night.

Sun light shone strongly through the car window as they drove to look at the first house. When they found it they saw that it was tiny. Its paint peeled off the sides and near the back it was black from fire and smoke. Through a hole in the door they could see there was no carpet inside and they didn't bother to call the real estate agent. Driving up to the next house they could see they didn't want it either. With the house being fifty years old it needed so much work they couldn't afford to pay for it all. The agent waited for them outside. "It needs new air conditioning and a door on the fence in the back yard."

Ashley could see holes in the walls. "It seems like everything in this house needs to be fixed. Let's just forget it."

Deanna nodded in agreement.

The next house they approached resembled an old fashioned hotel. "Do you like the looks of this house?" Ashley asked.

"Yes, let's call the number," Deanna answered. They both dialed it on their cell phone. The real estate office was only five minutes away. They arrived there and sat down at the desk.

"The house you're buying is 150 years old. Now when are you planning on moving in?" agent Sally asked.

"In about two or three months, after we finish packing and after she goes on vacation," Ashley answered.

"Okay that's great. Do you want the keys now?"

"Yes, that would be fine." After all of the paperwork was signed Sally Helms handed Ashley the keys. "Thank you."

Ashley handed a key to Deanna and they left the office to drive to the house.

When they entered the house they liked what they saw. "I wish we could stay here instead of at the motel." They both picked out which room they wanted. Deanna's had been on the right side of the house and Ashley's on the left with a guest room beside it.

"We should just go straight to the hospital instead of going back to the motel first. Let's go," Ashley walked out the front door. When Deanna joined her Ashley said, "Do you want to stay here?"

Deanna replied, "No." and got into the car.

They entered Beth's room and she was still awake. A doctor showed up. "She's got liver cancer. Now we want to take more tests."

"How much longer does she have to live?" Ashley asked crying her eyes out.

"I can only guess maybe a month. If she makes it through the next two days okay we can try chemotherapy and that might give her six months more to live." The doctor left the room.

"Thank you. Beth?" Ashley shook her. "The doctor is going to want your permission to start chemotherapy so will you be ready to sign?"

Beth nodded.

"Tomorrow I'll get your suitcase and bring everything to you. Do you want us to try to have you moved to a hospital in

Victorville?"

Beth nodded again.

"Deanna and I found a house. It's really old but we love it. I'm going to bring you your dinner now. Do you want anything else? How do you feel?"

"Don't bring me anything. I'm angry, but glad I'm dying then I won't have any more pain." She said this looking calm like she wasn't worried.

"Okay." Ashley and Deanna left the room and started walking towards the cafeteria.

Deanna woke again to the sound of Ashley knocking on her door.

"Hi Deanna, how are you feeling?"

"Not so good. I had been excited about the move until Beth got sick." Deanna's voice quivered.

"Cheer up. Beth's not going to die. She'll get lots of treatments I feel that she'll turn out to be a miracle. Why don't you smile and we'll go out now and check out the town."

"Okay." Deanna quickly got up.

"It doesn't seem to be much of a city. Whatever that means," Ashley said as they drove to what appeared to be a small mall.

"It looks like something that got built early last century. Maybe it did." The town resembled an old ghost town from the early west colored mostly in brown. "I like it here,"

Deanna said as she stepped up to the porch of what seemed to be a bar. Ashley followed her in through the door to get drinks. "We'll both have a beer." Deanna told the bartender. As Deanna waited for the drinks Ashley took a tourist guide and city map off the shelf, then placed them on the counter to buy. "After this let's go to our house and clean it up. I'll grab a towel and cleaner." Deanna nodded in agreement.

They entered their dirty and dusty house with a bag that
contained a six-pack of water, a new phone, and a glass vase of
flowers. Ashley placed the vase on the kitchen windowsill and
the phone in the jack. "The electricity should have been turned
on this morning and the phone company was also supposed to
turn the phone on. Our phone number is in the paper work for
this house. I'm going to plug in this phone and call Beth."
Ashley began dialing the hospital number and watched Deanna
wipe off dust. While on the phone Ashley threw away some
old newspaper in their grocery bag that got left on the floor.
Nobody answered Beth's phone so Ashley dialed the
hospital main number. "Is Beth Forester still in room 412?"
She hung up the phone. "Let's go visit Beth."

"I don't want to go I just can't take anymore. You go
ahead," Deanna answered.

"Okay I'll come back and get you, hopefully with Beth."

"Alright or maybe I'll just walk back to the motel," Deanna
answered as she watched Ashley walk out the door.
Ashley entered room 412 to find Beth gone. She walked
out to a front desk. "Can you tell me where Beth Forester is?"
The nurse looked up and answered, "No," as she shook her
head.

Ashley ran around the hospital looking for Beth. She ran to
the public restroom, the cafeteria, the gift room and when she
didn't find her there she ran out to the front of the building.
Beth couldn't be seen sitting anywhere outside. Ashley took
an elevator to the fourth floor where Beth's room had been.
Ashley sat down in room 412 but Beth couldn't be found
anywhere. Ashley sat and waited a few minutes to see if she
returned.

Picking up the phone she called the motel but Beth did not
answer. When it got dark and Beth didn't show Ashley
decided it was time to go pick Deanna up. She had waited long
enough.

Deanna sat waiting on the floor. The house looked clean.

"Let's go," Ashley said.

Deanna got up and they walked out to the car.

"I couldn't find Beth at the hospital. We'll go back
tomorrow and look for her again. She couldn't have
disappeared she was probably in another room having some
tests. Someone's going to know where is."

They drove back to the motel to spend the rest of the night.
They went to the hospital in the morning and entered
Beth's room looking for her. She was not there.
"I'm scared the only place we haven't checked is the
morgue should we go down there just to be sure," said Ashley.

They went down to the basement where the morgue was
and asked the attendant to check for Beth's name on his
records. The two girls almost fainted they were so glad to hear
the attendant say no he did not see her name on his paperwork.
"Walking up to the nurse's station Ashley asked, "Tell us
where is Beth Forester?"

The nurse responded, "One minute," and began checking
her computer. A screen with a listing of Beth Forester came
up. "She's in room 365 we had to move her yesterday because
her air conditioner broke down."

"Is she better?" Deanna asked.

"The doctor is with her now and everyone is amazed
because the treatments she received yesterday have really taken
affect. She looks and feels great. The doctor is calling her the
Miracle Girl and has released her to your custody as long as
she checks into the local hospital near her home." The nurse
did not look up and continued her work.

"Okay, that's terrific, thanks." Both ladies left the hospital
and drove to the motel to get their belongings. Then they
drove back to hospital to pick up Beth.

"Let's go home now," said Deanna as they helped Beth into
the back seat. It truly was a miracle and they all had big smiles
on their faces as they drove away.

Ashley stopped to call her mother, "Mom we're on our way home now and Beth is with us she is so much better wait until you see her. Don't cry mom."

Ashley hung up the phone and said, "My mom is going to fix up a room for Beth and she can stay there if the doctor says it's alright. Now we have to concentrate on getting Greg and his cousin arrested."

Chapter Eight

Deanna had to leave soon on her vacation to British
Columbia, Canada in a few days so at home and started to
pack. She sat down on her chair and looked through her tourist
guide to find places she wanted to visit there. Her vacation
would only be for a week.

Deanna was glad and excited about her vacation. She had
never been to British Columbia and badly wanted to go.
Deanna liked flying and always had dreamed of going to far off
places.
As Deanna sat in her room it grew dark at nightfall. Ashley
appeared in the doorway.

"Hi," Ashley said.

Deanna smiled at her. She then lit a couple of candles and
they lit up Ashley's face. She felt glad to see her friend's
pretty face looking happy.

"When I come back from British Columbia I'll bring you
back a souvenir."

"I'm so glad you're finally getting your vacation." Ashley
walked away.

Deanna wanted to call Greg before she left and talk to him
so she could be sure he wasn't going anywhere. Then she
wanted to call the police to see how close they were to
arresting Greg and his cousin for Sheryl's death. Suddenly she
heard shouting. The voice belonged to Deanna's mother and
by the sound Deanna could tell her mother had gotten drunk.

"It's not my fault!" Ashley could be heard shouting and a
door slammed hard. Ashley entered Deanna's room. "My
mother's drunk and acting violent. She didn't seem like
herself. I think she's becoming an alcoholic. Why is she
criticizing? I think she's trying to blame everyone including
herself for Sheryl's death. Ashley shut the door

"Do you want to sleep on the couch in here tonight?"

"Okay."

"I was going to call Greg to check up on him" Deanna said.

"Call the bastard. I don't care. I can't believe you're not
scared of him. I'm not afraid of that rat though."
Deanna called Greg, but didn't talk long. "I think he acted
a little strange. He didn't talk much and didn't seem to want
to." She laughed a little. "He sounded a little nervous. Maybe
freighted because he's afraid of the police. Who cares?"
Ashley got up to get sheets and blankets for the couch
while Deanna laid down and watched the wax from the candle
drip slowly.

Ashley entered the room and whispered. "I hope my
mother's not going crazy. When I was a young girl she was so
nice, I swear."

"I'll call you when I get there," Deanna said as she hugged
Ashley goodbye. She noticed a bruise on Ashley's face.

"What happened? Did your mother do that to you?"

"Yes, I'll be okay. I just want to get away from her. I put
my cross next to my bed. She'll sober up soon. I have just
had a frightening thought. What if she keeps drinking? She
hasn't gotten over Sheryl's death yet and she says she sees her
ghost walking around the house at night. I feel like I need to
get away from all of this. Would you mind if I moved to New
Mexico before you?"

"No, never, go ahead. Who's going to drive the furniture
truck?"

"I don't know. This house is starting to feel like a
dungeon. Bye."

"Bye, want me to call you every day?" Deanna asked.

"That would make me feel better, yes."

"Okay I will." Deanna went to her car and left the house.
She also wanted to get out of the house.

While on the plane Deanna felt concerned about Ashley.
She would call her every day to make sure she seemed okay.
The ride would take four hours to get to Vancouver, British
Columbia. Her attention became shifted from Ashley to her
vacation and she couldn't wait to see the nearby island where
she wanted to stay and go to the beach. She had just bought
herself a new sequined $200 bathing suit that she couldn't wait
to wear. Looking out of the window at the distant colorful
sight of the world Deanna fell asleep.

"Greg don't," Deanna screamed as he tied her up.

"No you're out of luck now," Greg screamed with an evil
smile.

Deanna screamed and the loud sound of screeching could
be heard. They both looked around for the noise but couldn't
see it. Greg lifted a knife to stab Deanna and she tensed up.
The sound started again and she clenched her fists before he
could hurt her and as Greg plunged his knife towards her
stomach she panicked. Then she woke up in her seat on the
plane.

Deanna heard the sound again she had heard in her dream.
The plane had been landing and she could feel it jerking as it
hit the ground and made the sound.

"Please stay in your seat with your seat belt fastened," a
woman's voice could be heard over a speaker as Deanna
opened her eyes to wake up.

Shortly the plane landed and people stood up to get off.
Deanna felt relieved and watched out the window glad it had
been only a dream. When most people had left she stood up to
get her purse and bag from the compartment above. Getting
off the plane she walked to the airport and got her suitcase.
Her motel was only a couple of blocks away and Deanna
began walking. "I'll rent a car when I'm ready to get to the
island." The Columbian motel appeared after only fifteen
minutes and she checked in.

First she called Ashley. "I'm fine. Are you?"

"Yes," Ashley answered.

"I'm excited so give me an idea what you want for a present?"

"I'll love anything you get," Ashley answered.

"I'm in the Columbian motel so call me if you need me. I'm in room 4B."

"Have a good night. I'll call you tomorrow, bye Barbie."

"Bye."

Deanna hesitated calling Greg. She thought, *Should I tell him about the dream?*

She heard his obnoxious, "Hello?"

"Greg?" She said really only calling him to make sure he didn't disappear. "It's me."

"Yes, Deanna? Are you enjoying Vancouver?"

"Yes, actually I just got here but I know I'm going to love it."

"I'm starting to miss you. Do you miss me?"

"I'd really rather not say. I was just glad to get away."

"Well I suppose you don't care anything about me."
That certainly was the truth. Deanna didn't care. He had been only a means to an end of a problem and Deanna hated problems. However, Greg was still not in jail.

"Did you know conflict can be unavoidable and it happens in the best of relationships?"

"That means I had a good relationship with Sheryl."

"Was that a bad joke? Greg, that isn't funny. I'm moving remember?"

"Maybe not for you but for me it is. Do you want to be my girlfriend? I think I love you."

"No Greg, I don't. I'm being honest."

"You're beautiful and sweet and I wish you were mine. Do I still get a going away date?"

"No, do you know where I am?"

"At the Columbian, room 4B. I could find you anywhere and force you to be with me."

"Stop it Greg or you'll wish you were in prison instead."

"Will you call me tomorrow Dean?"

"Maybe, I had a bad dream about you on the plane. Damn those dreams!"

"I'm sorry."

"I'll call to you tomorrow Dean. You know what I haven't seen Caleb in a long time."

"Bye Greg." Deanna hung up the phone and laid back and closed her eyes. She jumped when the phone rang and when she looked towards the window the sky was dark. She didn't know if she wanted to answer the phone she thought it might be Greg again. She stood up and turned on a light. The phone kept ringing so she answered. "Greg stop messing around!"

"Deanna it's me Ashley. I wanted to say good night and I hope you have a great time. Will you take pictures of the beach when you go?"

"Yes, anything for you."

"Thanks, my mother is acting quieter. I think she's trying to quit drinking. She also apologized to me for hitting me. I'll let you go now."

"Okay, I'm still tired so bye." Deanna hung up.
Deanna closed her eyes and fell asleep. Minutes later she appeared in a dark hallway in a dream. There was a bright light shining through a crack and she realized she stood in Ashley's basement. "Ashley!" Deanna called. No one

answered. Deanna could hear the sound of footsteps in the house. The sound came from Sheryl's room.

Sheryl came towards her down the hall. "Hi Deanna. You look good. I'm glad. I loved you and I wanted you to feel good. I'm so glad. I want to say one thing about Greg. He and Caleb were responsible for my death. You shouldn't see him again he's dangerous."

Deanna watched and dreamed of her late friend's affection and protection around her. Deanna shivered with fear as Sheryl's cold hand touched her.

"Goodbye Deanna, Sheryl said."
Deanna fearfully jumped back as Sheryl became a decomposing corpse and began walking towards her.

"Remember I'm not too far away ever. You know where I am," Sheryl said.
Sheryl called, "I'm watching over you."

Deanna woke and turned on the light. She felt shaken by the dream and decided to get dinner. There were restaurants down the road so Deanna left her room to walk to them. After leaving the restaurant Deanna saw a movie theatre and went inside. She bought a ticket to see a Romantic movie. Not many people were in the theatre. As she sat down a young man sat next to her. He bumped into her and spilled a soda on her.

"Oh I'm sorry miss, miss, what's your name?" He asked.

"Deanna Jennings." This man appeared young and full of life though Deanna would find he was not as young as he looked but a few years older than she was. "What's yours?"

"Ray Cooper, give me your number and I'll pay for any damages done to your clothes." Deanna immediately liked him and she nodded in agreement and began writing her number with a pen and paper she took out of her purse.

"I'll buy you a soda, okay?" Ray asked.

"Yes, I would like that." She handed him her number as the lights darkened and previews of movies started playing.

"You're not from around here are you? Where are you from?" he asked.

"Victorville, California but I'm moving with my best friend Ashley to Santa Fe, New Mexico. I thought I would really like it there but I'm not sure now and we've already bought a house. We were going through some problems together. See we've been friends for years and I had been ripped off by a travel agent. She wanted to stick up for me so when her sister went to confront the guy she never came home and she was found dead. We think we know who killed her. Now I have had to date the guy just to try and get him to confess to the police and not run away. Finally I got this vacation here out of him for credit on the one vacation he ripped me off

"Shhh, be quiet," came from some woman who had just entered the theatre and Deanna didn't want to talk any more. .

"Let's go get you a soda," Ray whispered as the movie started.

"Wait, I don't want to miss the beginning." He agreeably sat and watched with her. The more attention he paid to her the more she felt attracted to him.

When the movie was almost over she said, "I've seen enough let's go now." They both got up and left the movie theatre.

"I wrote down my motel phone number and my number in California. I'm going to try to find a way to get out of moving to New Mexico right now. I think I'll try and put it off for a while."

"That's good. Let me give you my number and we'll go do something together tomorrow."

"Okay I wanted to go to the beach."

"Fine we'll do that," he answered.

"I definitely want to go shopping so you could help me pick out a souvenir for Ashley."

"Okay," it's a date he answered.

"Is it supposed to be a date?" Deanna asked.
"Yes."

"Okay that's fine. You can call me Dean or maybe Dee if you want to."

"Alright, I'll walk you home. It's dark."
They both entered the motel lobby together. "What time should I come by tomorrow?"

"How about ten in the morning?"

"Great," Ray answered.

"Okay, tomorrow will be my last day here then I'm going to Vancouver Island."

"I can meet you there. Could I take you there? And when you're leaving I can take you to the airport too."

"That's great." Ray stood next to the door to leave. "I'll see you tomorrow morning." He left. Deanna went to her room and sat on the bed realizing she already liked Ray. She wanted to get rid of Greg forever, but for now because justice for Sheryl seemed so necessary she had to see Greg occasionally. If Sheryl died defending Deanna then Deanna wanted to repay her. She hopped the police would hurry up and put Greg away. She felt very attracted to Ray for sure and wanted to keep in touch with him after she left the area. If Greg knew that she thought he would be upset.

Deanna peeled off her soda-covered clothes. She knew soda probably wouldn't stain and wondered why he offered to pay for them. Getting into the shower to refresh herself she couldn't stop thinking about Ray.
After going to bed early Deanna woke to the sun rising.
She opened her window to hear the sound of birds chirping like they seemed to do every morning like a rooster announcing the sunrise.

When she finished eating breakfast Ray came to knock on the door. She answered it.

"Hi, come in. What is your last name?"

"Hill."

"Will you write to me after I leave? I won't be here long?" She asked.

"Yes, I promise. Are you ready?" Ray asked.

"I am. Let's go." Deanna picked up her purse and left the room. They both walked out to the parking lot.

"This is my car." Ray pointed to a brown four door Chevy. He opened the door. "Get in." Deanna stepped in and sat down.

They rode for thirty minutes before she saw the beach. It looked like any other beach she had seen on the Pacific coast. He parked the car and they both got out. "I want to collect sea shells for Ashley." She walked to the sand where the tide rolled in and she began picking up sand dollars and small shells. She stared out at the horizon temped to toss the shells back but didn't. It started to feel romantic.

"Get down here Ray!" she said, invitingly. She sat down on the sand as he approached her. He sat down next to her. She took off her shoes and tossed them back to put her feet out to reach the water.

"Tell me about you. How old are you?"

"I'm twenty five. I was born and raised here. I live by my self in Vancouver and work as a car salesman."

"That sounds interesting. I'm twenty-one, I told you where I'm from and I'm into retail work but I want to be a social worker. I don't have a boyfriend." She smiled. "I don't want today to be the last day I see you."

"You can spend the night tonight then I'll take you to the island." Ray invited her.

"I want to but I feel like I can't get enough of you and I'll have four nights left here. Stay in the motel at the island with me, please. You would have your own room."

"Of course I want to." The smile on his face seemed to invite Deanna and she kissed him on the lips.

"I'm falling in love with you. I swear," Deanna confessed. He said nothing as they both sat in the sand and relaxed.

"Alright let's go shopping." He agreeably stood up so they could walk to the car. Knowing what waited for her in California she did not ever want to leave Canada.
While riding in his car she added, "I'm hoping to come back to this area, then we could see each other again. Do you want to see me again? Do you like me at all?" She put her hand on his shoulder to invite him to ask her out as he nodded. He thought she was a little too honest. Five minutes later they were at a small shopping strip. He stopped the car and she could see there were gift shops.

"I want to get Ashley a souvenir." She stepped into a gift shop.

They soon left the shop with a small box of post cards and a key chain that said British Columbia.

"Why don't you come back to my house?" asked Ray.

"I want to call Ashley before I forget," Deanna answered.

"You can do that at my house."

"Okay, let's go."

Ten minutes later they pulled up to a large Victorian style house two level home. She stepped out of the car and he opened the front door and motioned her to come in. She followed him in and sat down on a brown velvety couch.

"Can I get you something to drink?" he asked.

"Yes anything is okay."

Ray went into the kitchen and came back with a soda. "I'd like to learn the history of this country. Let's go to a museum."

"Okay we can do that tomorrow at Victoria Island I'm sure. I want to ask you to spend the night."

"You know my clothes are back at the motel and I'm paid for tonight." Looking at him Deanna felt so attracted to him she thought she might have felt lust and just wanted him around. "Why don't you spend the night at my motel room?"

"Yes, that would be alright."
Ray went to pack his clothes for a few days. "Here's the phone." He handed Deanna the phone.

"What's that for?" she asked.

Ray smiled at her forgetfulness. "So you can call Ashley." As if remembering she took the phone and started dialing Ashley's number.

She turned her attention to the phone. "Hello I'm sitting here with a handsome man and I'm having a good time. Please tell me your okay."

"No I'm not," Ashley answered.

"Okay is this because of Greg or some new crap I haven't heard?" Deanna asked.

"My mother hasn't been home in days."

"Don't worry I'll be home in less than a week. I've met someone his name is Ray. He and I are going back to the motel now. I'll call you when we get to the island."
Deanna hung up the phone then asked, "Are you ready?"
Looking around the house she saw she liked it maybe enough to stay there forever. Ray began heading towards the door. She walked out to the car waiting for him. While riding in the car she wondered what they would do the rest of the night, if they would drive each other crazy, or would she think of a way for them to be together forever.

They entered her motel room. At that time she noticed how small it really was. "I know it's small. Let's go swimming until dinner." They both agreed. She put on some shorts and a tank top because she didn't feel like wearing a bathing suit in front of him.

Out at the pool she jumped in the water and he followed her wearing only shorts. "Do you want to go back to California with me she asked?"

"Wow you don't waste any time do you. I would like to do that. I just don't think it will happen. We could be together for a few days."

Deanna nodded in agreement but didn't really want to take him back to California because of Greg. She still had to keep in touch with him.

"Deanna lets go a little slower. Let's not rush into a relationship to quickly."

"Okay, we were lucky meeting the way we did," Deanna said as she got up to go to a chair to lie in the sun. She closed her eyes and listened to the sound of Ray splashing in the water.

Suddenly she saw Ashley standing beside her. "Hi Dean," Ashley said with a smile. Ashley just kept grinning. "I miss you and can't wait for you to get back."

"Ashley, I brought you a souvenir."

"Okay that's good. I can't wait for us to move to Santa Fe. I want to swim. What's wrong? Do you want me to kill Greg for you?" Ashley said as she stopped smiling but looked aggressive. "I can do it you know. Come on, do you want me to or not? I want to know."

"Ashley?" Deanna sat up frightened at what she heard and opened her eyes. Ray looked at her. "Was I sleeping?"

"Yeah you fell asleep and I heard you say 'Ashley'?"

"Oh," she answered and saw she had been lying directly in the hot summer sun and turning pink. "I should have brought sun tan lotion. I'm going in." She walked into the room with the door locked and turned on the TV listening for Ray's knock.

At the island Deanna could see the beach from her motel window. Ray and Deanna did not share a room but stayed in rooms right next to each other. She approached his door and knocked, he answered. "What are you up to nothing?"

"I want to go gambling or to a summer carnival," Ray answered.

"In this heat?" The summer the temperature hit 110 degrees in the sun.

"Just for a little while. I'll be back in an hour." Deanna watched as Ray left the motel area.

At the carnival he felt like he didn't want to stay. There were games for children and he didn't know what made him want to go there. Suddenly in his heart he felt his affection for Deanna grow. Leaving the area he walked over to a gift shop and saw a stand on the counter of beautiful rings. He picked one out to give to Deanna as a loving going away present and at the nearby drug store he picked up a Coke and a dozen red roses. She had to leave in three days.

Deanna answered the door when he knocked and he stood there with the ring box in his hand and flowers. "This is a symbol of my affection." He handed her the gifts.
She didn't really know what to say and, "Oh thank you," came out. He nodded and she invited him in. As he sat down she asked, "Are you going to California with me?"

"No," he answered.

"Could you please tell me why not?" she asked.

"There are reasons I don't want to point out but it's not because I don't care about you. I have no intentions of living in California." Deanna took the ring out of the box and put it on.

"I promise you I'll write to you and call you," Ray said. Deanna still didn't really want to leave. "What do you think of me moving here? Maybe I could." She decided she would look at local malls and real estate companies in her remaining days there.

"Alright if you need my help just ask," Ray answered.

"Let's have lunch at the nearby sandwich shop." She nodded and they left the room to eat.

When Deanna came back the sky began darkening and she sat alone. She could hear the sound of the ocean rolling on and off the shore. The room became quiet except for the ocean. She lay down on the bed as the room darkened. Slam! A crashing sound obviously came from Ray's room. She sat up wondering if the sound was caused by an accident or if he has banged into the wall. To be sure he was alright and see that he didn't have a serious problem she went to knock on his door to check.

When no one answered the door she tried the knob. The door was open. The knob turned but the door didn't open.

"Deanna!" She heard him shout.

"Yeah, I'm here. I'm trying to get this door open. Are you okay?" she asked.

"Yes."

"I heard a bang." Deanna tried shoving the door but when it wouldn't open she became frustrated and started beating the door. Suddenly it slid open. Surprised she saw Ray looking at her. "What was that bang I heard?"

"I don't know either. It sounded like it was coming from the inside walls. Maybe it was thunder. Do you want to move to a different motel? We still have two nights here."

"I'm not sure. Why don't you stay with me tonight? I'll sleep on the couch."

He agreed and took his suitcase and followed her to her room. They both lay down. "I don't want to leave," Deanna said.

"I can look for a place for you to live and send you information," Ray said staring up at the dark ceiling.

They rested and slept a lot during the next two days. They didn't say much but were brought closer together. It was suddenly time for Deanna to leave. They were at the airport in Vancouver and were ready to say goodbye. "Bye Deanna. I'll call and write to you and email you. If you want to move to British Columbia let me know and I'll let you stay in my house until you find your own place."

"Really, are you serious?" Deanna felt excited about Ray's invitation. "I'll think about it. I really want to, but I have to see if I can arrange it. I can't wait to see Ashley again. Do you want to see her picture?" She opened her wallet and showed him a picture of all the Forester sisters. "Bye," she said and gave him a hug sadly disappearing through the door.

She took her seat on the plane and it lifted up into the air after she put on a seat belt. She swore to herself, *I'm not falling asleep and dreaming about Greg this time.* She dozed off a few times but had been entertained by magazines most of the time.

When she landed she called Ashley on the phone. Deanna felt excited to hear Ashley's voice again.
Ashley sounded excited also. "I'm making spaghetti for dinner."

Deanna jumped in gladness at the idea. Spaghetti was always one of her favorite foods, that and Mexican.
Deanna couldn't decide what she wanted to do. It would be difficult to decide if it would better to live in New Mexico with her best friend or cohabit with Ray in British Columbia.

Deanna wouldn't be in the states anymore and eventually she thought she would probably want to come back. The future still looked murky and dark to her because she had wasn't glad to be moving to New Mexico and the Greg Wager problem still wasn't solved.

Deanna quickly headed back home. Ashley sat on the couch and watched her. The house seemed cozier than it ever did before. She dropped her suitcase down in her room and put

Ashley's gift down in front of her. "Didn't I tell you I'd bring you a present?"

Ashley studied it with her eyes. "Let's eat dinner now. Thanks for remembering me. I don't know where my mother is and I'm worried."

They both sat down at the dinner table. "I've practically gotten Greg to confess to murder and not make excuses. He and his cousin are the killers. You know sometimes it's got to be just so hard to prove a crime like murder. He looks all sweet and innocent on the outside but on the inside, I'm sure there are skeletons and cobwebs. He's a total weirdo."

From all of the excitement she felt nervous. "I told you about the man I met his name is Ray, well he says I can stay with him. I don't think I can do that even though I liked him very much and this is where my home is. I'll call him and keep in touch, but I think after a time he won't want to be with me anymore." Most of the lights were out in the house. Candles were lit giving short distances of light. The still seemed cozy but yet a little spooky to them.

"How soon do you think we can move?" Deanna asked.

"In a month or so. We want to be there when school starts."

www.ingramcontent.com/pod-product-compliance
Lightning Source LLC
Chambersburg PA
CBHW020631130626
46552CB00003B/1172